# If
# This
# Were
## a
# Story

# If This Were a Story

## Beth Turley

*Simon & Schuster Books for Young Readers*

NEW YORK LONDON TORONTO SYDNEY NEW DELHI

SIMON & SCHUSTER BOOKS FOR YOUNG READERS
An imprint of Simon & Schuster Children's Publishing Division
1230 Avenue of the Americas, New York, New York 10020
Excerpts on pages 39, 71, 99, 135, 180, 195, and 233 from LOST IN THE FUNHOUSE
by John Barth, copyright © 1963, 1966, 1968, 1969 by John Barth.
Used by permission of Doubleday, an imprint of the Knopf DoubledayPublishing Group,
a division of Penguin Random House LLC. All rights reserved.
SIMON & SCHUSTER BOOKS FOR YOUNG READERS
is a trademark of Simon & Schuster, Inc.
For information about special discounts for bulk purchases, please contact Simon & Schuster
Special Sales at 1-866-506-1949 or business@simonandschuster.com.
The Simon & Schuster Speakers Bureau can bring authors to your live event. For more
information or to book an event, contact the Simon & Schuster Speakers Bureau at
1-866-248-3049 or visit our website at www.simonspeakers.com.
Also available in a Simon & Schuster Books for Young Readers hardcover edition
Cover design by Krista Vossen
Interior design by Hilary Zarycky
The text for this book was set in Bodoni Std.
Manufactured in the United States of America
0819 OFF
First Simon & Schuster Books for Young Readers paperback edition September 2019
2 4 6 8 10 9 7 5 3 1
The Library of Congress has cataloged the hardcover edition as follows:
Names: Turley, Beth, author.
Title: If this were a story / Beth Turley.
Description: First edition. | New York : Simon & Schuster Books for Young Readers, [2018] |
Summary: Ten-year-old Hannah copes with the bullies at school and trouble at home through the
power of her imagination.
Identifiers: LCCN 2017043725 | ISBN 9781534420618 (hardcover : alk. paper) |
ISBN 9781534420625 (pbk) | ISBN 9781534420632 (eBook)
Subjects: | CYAC: Imagination—Fiction. | Bullying—Fiction. | Family problems—Fiction. |
Middle schools—Fiction. | Schools—Fiction.
Classification: LCC PZ7.1.T875 If 2018 | DDC [Fic]—dc23
LC record available at https://lccn.loc.gov/2017043725

To my family

# If
# This
# Were
# a
# Story

# The Note

I measure how happy a day is with sounds. Happy days sound like a TV on low volume or birdcalls through a screen door. Sad days sound like dishes crashing into each other in the sink. Sad days sound like too-loud voices. Once a day is stained sad, it's hard to make it happy again.

My class copies vocabulary into our notebooks. I write the words like an astronomer discovering a new planet, as if the definitions can unlock the secrets of outer space. "Instantaneous": when something happens without any delay. "Iridescent": the quality of changing colors when viewed from different angles. "Intention": an aim or a plan.

The tip of my pencil breaks. I walk to the back of the room and shove my pencil into the sharpener. The grinding sound is a happy one. It means a new point, a shiny do-over.

On the way back to my desk, I see a small piece of paper crunched into a ball on the floor. I pick the paper up with the *intention* of throwing it away, but it looks like my name is written on it. I unravel the note and read the three words on a torn sheet of lined paper. The words fill my head with the sound of flying arrows, quiet and quick and aimed in my direction. A sad-day sound.

NOBODY LIKES HANNAH.

# Pine-Tree Hugs

I don't know what to do with the note. I keep it tucked in my hand and sit back at my desk with thoughts as loud as fireworks in my brain. *Nobody likes me? What did I do?* A new piece of paper slides across my desk. Courtney watches me, pointing her chin to the new note. I open it.

WHAT'S WRONG?

Before I understand what my hands are doing, I rip up Courtney's note and stuff the pieces into my desk. I should tell my best friend about what I found, but I would rather the note just disappeared. What if she sees those words and believes them?

"Hand it over, Hannah," a voice demands from behind me. I turn to find my teacher, Mrs. Bloom, with an outstretched palm, tapping her rubber shoe.

"I don't have anything," I answer. I've made a mistake. I shouldn't have picked up the note.

"You know the rules." Her long dress is covered in roses, with thorns still attached to the green stems.

3

I focus on the printed flowers by her ankles and drop the note into her hand. A little cough rises from her throat.

"Keep copying, everyone. Hannah, come with me."

I try not to notice my classmates staring while Mrs. Bloom takes me into the hallway. We stop a few feet from the door, and I focus on the walls. Our introduction bulletin board from the first day of school is still hanging up. I reread my "About Me":

HI, I'M HANNAH. I'M A SPELLING BEE CHAMPION WHO LIKES STORIES AND SOUNDS.

I remember completing the assignment and wondering how anyone could narrow themselves down to just one sentence, as if there weren't a million *iridescent* facets of a person to look at, like a prism in the sun.

I should've written: I'M HANNAH, AND NOBODY LIKES ME.

"Hannah?" Mrs. Bloom waves her hand in front of my face.

"Yes?"

"Who gave this to you?"

4

"I found it on the floor."

Mrs. Bloom taps her rubber shoe again. She has an "About Me" on the bulletin board too. It says: *Hi, I'm Mrs. Bloom. I'm a fifth-grade teacher who likes playing with my cats.*

"Do you have any idea who would write this?" she asks. I stare at the floor until it turns to a soft gray blur.

"If nobody likes me, then I guess it could be anybody."

She puts the note into the pocket of her dress and touches my shoulder.

"That's not true, Hannah. Everything is going to be fine." We walk back into the room together, and my whole class watches me. My chair scrapes the tiles on the floor when I go to sit down, and makes a sad-day sound that echoes forever.

My heart beats hard like a drum for the last hour of the school day, and I can't slow it down. I worry about palpitations, the uneven rhythm of my heart's beating. I try to spell the word "palpitation" with each new thump, but only get to *p-a-l-p* before I'm spelling the words from the note instead. *L-i-k-e-s.*

5

The note is a palpitation, and I don't know how to set things straight again, how to get the music in my heart back on track.

I'm still shaky when I walk home from school. I like my walks home, because I learn how months feel. October is like sinking into cool water, but the good kind of cool water that makes you feel awake. The best sounds are hidden inside October air, inside the smell of chimney smoke and cold. A song from a chorus of shivering leaves. The whisper of a secret-keeping wind.

If I listen hard enough, the world speaks to me. I hear magic the same way I hear happy and sad day sounds, but the mysterious voices are always just beyond my reach, not focused enough for me to really understand. There's something the sounds want to tell me, I just know it, but they're still too quiet. I hope someday my dormant powers will wake up and make everything better.

My house is so close to school that I can practically see the school from my front porch, so the walk doesn't take too long. Dad's truck is in the driveway. He's usually not home till dark. I *instantaneously* feel like a girl made of quicksand.

I open the front door and see Dad on the couch. His hands are covered in white paint and balled up in his lap. The TV is on, loud. A knife slaps the cutting board too hard in the kitchen. Sad-day sounds.

"Hi, Dad." I stay close to the door, where I can escape to the front yard and suck down October air if the yelling picks up where it left off last night.

Not even the rain against the roof drowned out the fight. Not even my pillow.

"How was your day?" Dad asks but doesn't look away from the TV.

"It was okay. Why are you home?"

He takes a sip from his Coke. I flinch when he drops the can back down onto the table.

"When you build houses for people, they can change their minds. And you lose hundreds of dollars and weeks of your time."

I'm not made of quicksand anymore. I'm a chemical reaction. Motion sickness mixes with panic and adds in a few drops of melancholy, but I don't let Dad see.

7

"I'm sorry," I say.

Mom comes into the room with a towel in her hands and hair piled high in a bun. I can tell how Mom is feeling by how tightly her bun is tied. Today it's a mess of black frizz and flyaways.

"Hannah, is there something you want to tell us?" she asks.

*I heard you fight last night. It sounded like thunder.*

*"I'm sick of being responsible for making all the money here," Dad yelled.*

*"I stay home to take care of Hannah," Mom yelled back.*

*"She can start taking care of herself."*

I blink hard, my way of escaping when I get too stuck in yesterdays.

"What do you mean?" I ask.

"I just got an email from your teacher. Are you being bullied?"

Dad looks at me with eyes like concerned spotlights. All the anger in them disappears. The science experiment inside me settles down a little.

"I found a note. It was . . . mean," I tell them.

"What did the note say?" Dad asks.

"It said that nobody likes me."

There's no yelling or cutting board slapping or door slamming. The only sound is the ticking clock on the mantel. A sound more happy than sad, because it's quiet.

Dad crosses the room to wrap me in his arms. His hug smells like cut wood, like a pine tree. I breathe it in. The chalky white paint on his shirt brushes my cheek.

"No one says that to my girl. No one bullies you," Dad says urgently.

*Bullies.* I have the basic definition in my brain dictionary. I add more.

Bullying hurts as much as a punch in the face, even if it doesn't touch you. Bullying makes you forget about everything except being whole and safe and happy again.

Maybe Dad wants me to be safe more than he wants to be angry. I close my eyes; I would want to find another hundred notes if it meant Dad would hold me in his pine-tree hug where no storm could touch us again. I'd do anything to make the sad sounds go quiet forever.

# Ambrose the Stuffed Elephant

That night I slip into bed and pull Ambrose my stuffed elephant toward me. I hold him tight and compose wishes that might make him speak, like I have every night since Dad gave him to me. That was two years ago. There was something about his black bead eyes that generated light. The moon through my window hit the top of his head like a lopsided halo and made me believe in guardian angels (well, guardian elephants). I haven't gotten Ambrose to talk to me yet, but something tells me not to quit.

Ambrose is named after a character in a story called "Lost in the Funhouse." Ms. Meghan, the school counselor I used to see, told me she knew I liked big vocabulary and gave me the story to read. She told me that she'd taken out the parts I was too young for and that I might not understand it all, but I should give it a try. I didn't really understand it then, but I thought about it all the time. In the story the narrator keeps reminding you that it's a story. It's like the story knows itself too well, and I think that was the problem with the character Ambrose. He knew too much and thought too much, so his head was all full and he got lost. I told this to Ms. Meghan when we met again. She nodded and scribbled in her notebook and asked if that reminded me of anyone. I said no.

If this were a story like "Lost in the Funhouse," then the note I found on the floor would be the inciting incident that sets everything into motion, like the discovery of a body in a murder mystery. I would be the lead detective in a trench coat and brown hat, propelling the narrative forward by uncovering clues on my way toward finding the truth.

But this is not a story.

I sink my head into the pillow.

"Wake up, Ambrose," I whisper to his trunk, lifting him up into the air. "Wake up, wake up." I find the place inside where I think my magic hides and send it all to him.

And I swear, I swear, I swear, I see him blink.

"Whoa, put me down, sister," Ambrose says. Ambrose, *my stuffed elephant,* says.

11

I toss him across the room. He bounces against the dresser and lands facedown on the floor.

"Ouch," he cries, but he doesn't move. I'm stunned, ready to hide under my sheets. Ambrose's voice should be the happiest sound of them all, but instead I wonder why he chose tonight to speak up.

I crawl out of bed and lean Ambrose against the dresser, then sit cross-legged in front of him.

"I can hear you," I say.

"I'm happy to be heard." His mouth doesn't move when he speaks. He sounds like an elephant if an elephant could speak English, a rough and shouty sort of sound.

"Why did you wake up now?" I ask.

"You had a hard day," Ambrose replies.

"How do you know?"

"Because I know you, Hannah."

I listen for noises on the other side of the door, but there's only the creaking of the house. I move closer to Ambrose.

"What should I do about the note?" I ask.

"I can't tell you that," he replies.

I guess magic doesn't mean getting all the answers.

If a character in a story solves the puzzle on page one, why would you even keep reading?

"Do you think it's true that nobody likes me?"

"I like you."

I pull my legs in close and lean my face onto my knees. When I close my eyes, I see torn pieces of paper.

"They didn't fight tonight, you know," I say very matter-of-factly.

"I can't remember the last time that happened. And I'm an elephant. Our memories are exceptional," Ambrose says.

"I hope it's not because I was bullied. I don't want to be bullied anymore."

"Maybe your parents are just as tired of the sad sounds as you are."

"You know about the happy and sad sounds?" I ask. I don't think I've told Ambrose about the special way I hear the world.

"I told you, Hannah. I know you."

My eyelids start to lower against my will and I yawn. I pretend that this is a story where if I fall asleep, the world will end. I resist the tiredness with all my strength.

"Don't fight it. You should get some rest," Ambrose says.

"But you've just come to life."

"I'm not going anywhere."

I lift Ambrose toward me and squeeze his soft gray body.

"Hannah. Too tight," Ambrose wheezes. I laugh and tuck us into bed.

"Ambrose, why did you get lost in the funhouse?" I ask him before closing my eyes.

"I'm an elephant, silly. I've never been in a funhouse."

He hums a lullaby until I fall asleep.

# Acts of Kindness

When I walk into class the next morning, all the desks have a piece of lined paper on top of them. Mrs. Bloom stands in front of the room. The word "BULLYING" is written in red marker on the whiteboard behind her. I stop short, and Courtney runs into me.

"Watch out, Hannah," she says in the voice she uses when something annoys her.

"Sorry," I say in the voice I use to act like nothing's wrong.

Everyone sits down, pulls out a pencil, and writes their name on top of the paper, like we've been trained to do since kindergarten.

"Mrs. Bloom, is this a pop quiz?" Rebecca Snow asks hopefully. Rebecca loves quizzes of all kinds.

"No, it's an activity. An important one. There's been some bullying in this class, and it's not acceptable."

I stare so hard at the piece of paper that the blue lines on it disappear.

"What kind of bullying?" Courtney asks from the desk next to me.

"One of your classmates found a note with a hurtful comment, the kind of comment that could really damage someone's self-esteem."

She might as well say my name. Anyone who saw me walk into the hall with her yesterday is staring at me anyway. Like Courtney.

"Today we are going to do the opposite," Mrs. Bloom says. "Everyone rip your piece of paper in half." Mrs. Bloom rips her own piece as an example.

The room fills with tearing sounds that cut straight to my core.

"I'm going to have you pull one of your classmate's names out of a shoe box. On one of your pieces of paper, you're going to write something kind about the person you pick. When you're done, bring it to me."

Everyone looks sort of confused when they pull a name from the shoe box and start to write. Mrs. Bloom gives me a small smile when I pick out mine. I unfold the piece of paper and see KIMMY DOBSON written on it.

I try to think of something nice about Kimmy, but it feels like coming up with a story, a piece of make-believe. Kimmy is big and mean and draws circles in the dirt around the best swing at recess so that no one except her can use it. She's also my only real competition in the annual school spelling bee, because she's so good at spelling big words. Maybe she'd like to hear that. I write KIMMY IS A STUPEN-DOUS S-P-E-L-L-E-R on my paper and bring it up to Mrs. Bloom at the whiteboard.

When all the notes are handed in, Mrs. Bloom tapes them to the board and erases the word "BULLYING."

"Come up and see the great things your class-mates have to say. This is how we wipe bullying away, one act of kindness at a time."

We all clump together to look at the board.

COURTNEY WEARS CUTE CLOTHES.

REBECCA IS REALLY SMART.

THEO PLAYS BASKETBALL LIKE HE'S IN THE NBA.

I find my note toward the edge of the board.

I THINK HANNAH IS A GOOD PERSON.

The words make me feel a little brighter inside. Sometimes I think it's harder to be a good person than any other good thing. It's nice to know someone sees that I try, even if I don't know who they are.

"I hope you'll all keep choosing to be kind like you were on this board." Mrs. Bloom directs us back to our seats.

"What is the other piece of paper for?" Rebecca asks, probably still hoping for a quiz.

"The second half is for you to tell me what you know about any bullying notes. You don't have to write your name, but if you've seen something or heard something or know anything at all about who wrote the note, this is the time to speak up."

The room fills with shifting sounds. I look around and see some people glancing at Kimmy, because whenever there's bullying going on, she's usually the one behind it.

When Kimmy's mom died last year, Kimmy didn't come to school for two weeks. On the day of her return, we gave her a card with all our names signed inside. I saw her at recess that afternoon, digging a hole in the dirt when she thought no one was looking. She dropped torn-up pieces of the card inside her hole and then covered it back up. I wanted to tell Kimmy that I understood why she would bury the card, and that I knew what it was like to hide memories down deep—if only I could get within five feet of her without being hit by hate-rays. I never said anything.

I don't know if Kimmy wrote the note I found yesterday. All I know for sure is that it made me want to change everything unlikable about myself, even though I can't be anything but Hannah Geller. If I write that on my piece of paper, Mrs. Bloom will know it came from me. Instead I write I DON'T KNOW ANYTHING and drop the paper into Mrs. Bloom's shoe box.

When we grab our things from the shelves before lunch, Courtney punches my arm.

"The note was about you, wasn't it? That's what you talked to Mrs. Bloom in the hall about yesterday?" she asks in a low voice.

"Yeah," I whisper into my backpack.

"What did it say?"

"That nobody likes me."

Courtney sort of laughs. "That's not true, Hannah."

"Really?" I ask.

"I mean, you're not the most popular, but I still love you."

I know Courtney doesn't mean to make me feel as tiny as the note made me feel, or hollow like when Mom and Dad fight, but she does. I guess Courtney isn't the one who thinks I'm a good person.

# Lockdown Sounds

Cafeteria sounds aren't happy or sad, just clamorous. I sit with Courtney and Ryan at our blue table.

"Hey, Ryan, did you hear? Someone wrote a note about Hannah, and she didn't even tell us," Courtney announces before sucking on her organic-juice box. She's smaller and cuter than I am, with sun-colored hair and pink glasses. Usually I feel lucky that we're friends, because I'm the only fifth-grade girl sprouting zits. But when her mean side comes out, I don't feel lucky at all.

"What are you talking about?" Ryan asks, but he's looking at me.

"It only happened yesterday. And it wasn't a big deal," I answer.

"You know Hannah likes to keep secrets," Courtney continues.

Ryan reaches across the table and grabs my peach cup. He holds it in the air.

"I'm taking this peach cup prisoner until you tell us if you're okay."

"I've got the sandwich." Courtney slides my ham-and-cheese away.

If there were anyone in the world I could spill my feelings to like a tipped-over ink bottle, it would be Courtney and Ryan, my best friends since the alphabet sat us next to each other in kindergarten (Geller, Gilmore, and Grant). I like the idea that letters brought the three of us together. But I'd rather s-t-a-r-v-e than talk about the n-o-t-e anymore.

"I'm okay."

"Oh, really?" Ryan asks all mysteriously, with a mouth full of sloppy joe.

"Chew with your mouth closed, Ryan." Courtney wrinkles her nose.

"Are you my mother?"

"That's a book, not a question," I say.

The three of us jump when the cafeteria doors slam shut. I'm thankful for the distraction, until the lights go dark and the lunch monitors start running around to the tables.

"Have a happy day, Brookview Elementary." The

voice from the loudspeaker falls over the cafeteria like the start of nighttime.

The monitors herd us into groups around the edges of the cafeteria. I sink to the ground with my back against the wall. The lunch ladies seal themselves up in the kitchen. Ryan breathes shaky breaths next to me, so I reach for his hand, dark brown and very warm. Holding Ryan's hand feels funny but safe.

"What's happening?" he asks.

"It must be a lockdown drill. Those are the code words." I swallow down being scared to sound strong instead.

"But they always tell us when we're having one."

"I know."

"Does that mean it's real?" Courtney whispers.

"I don't know."

Footsteps echo in the hallway. The cafeteria doors rattle, and Courtney hides her face behind my arm. I breathe in deeply. The smell of sloppy joe and sanitizer makes my stomach twist into a knot.

This doesn't feel like a drill. I decide that drills are useless. Everything is different when the enemies aren't imaginary. No drill could prepare my heart to beat so wildly.

I wait for the ten years of my life to flash by, but instead I think about *Are You My Mother?* A baby bird is sent tumbling from its nest and into a desperate search for someone to love him. I always wondered why mama bird was who the baby bird belonged to, just because she was the same species. Maybe the dog or the bulldozer would have loved him just as much.

Undecipherable voices leak through the wall. I close my eyes and wait for whatever is out in the hall-ways to find us.

"We're clear," the loudspeaker says.

Like a miracle, the lights are turned back on. Relief floods all the way into my toes. If I listen hard enough, I can hear the calm crash over the cafeteria like a waterfall.

"Stay seated, everyone," Bubby, the head lunch monitor, shouts to the cafeteria.

Courtney peeks out from behind my arm. Ryan lets go of my hand like he was never scared at all.

"I knew it," he says.

Bubby whistles through his fingers to regain our attention.

"This was a lockdown drill. We must practice so that you know how to respond to an unexpected threat in the school. If you are alone and hear that announcement, get to the closest place to hide out of sight." Bubby waves us back to our seats.

I would like to tell Principal Jenkins that "have a happy day" is not an appropriate code for a lockdown, because lockdowns are full of sad-day sounds.

My friends and I turn ourselves from puddles of fear back into fifth graders, into the oldest students at Brookview Elementary. Liquid to solid. Phase transition.

Ryan fills his mouth with sloppy joe again.

"Where were we?" he mumbles through the goop.

"Gross," Courtney says, but she laughs.

I laugh too and pretend the world is still spinning the same way, but it's not. Somehow I've lost my center of gravity. The drill makes Ryan and Courtney move on from the note and start discussing the fall festival on Friday, so I take back my peach cup and sandwich. It's easier not to talk about things.

# From Mrs. Bloom's Shoe Box

I bet Kimmy did it.

I saw the note on the floor, but I
didn't pick it up.

I apologize, Mrs. Bloom, but I do
not know about the note. Signed,
Rebecca Snow

Courtney is a bully. She did it.

What did the note say?

I think the note was about Hannah.
That's all I have to say about it.
~Courtney

I hope whoever did it stops.

I'm hungry. From Theo.

It was Kimmy. End of story.

IDK

I liked the kind-words activity.

Sorry.

If I tell you who did it, will I get an
A?

Maybe Joanie? I know she's mad
that people were making fun of her.-
Katherine

I don't know anything.

You rock, Mrs. Bloom.

# Truth Serum

I have a pen pal. Her name is Ashley and she's in eighth grade. Getting a new letter from her is like Christmas, only better, because the present is made of words.

Today Mrs. Bloom looks at me for an extra second when she gives me my letter. I know she's worried about me because of the note, but I would like to forget about it. It feels better to forget than make lists in my head of the reasons why nobody likes me.

But the truth is, I don't forget anything. Even the things I wish I could.

I tear open the letter from Ashley and smooth it out on my desk. Ashley's handwriting looks like bubbles, and she dots her *I*s with circles. One time I tried to replicate the way she wrote on a blank sheet of paper. I couldn't catch on to the round-dotted *I*s and loopy *A*s. It's very hard to be something you're not.

The letter says:

Hey, Hannah,

Hope you're having a great day. Thanks for sending that cool vocabulary list with your last letter. I'm sure you'll do fine in your spelling bee. You could definitely beat me.

Are you excited about Halloween? I am. I don't go trick-or-treating anymore, but there is this party. Me and my friends are going as old-school pop stars, and I'm going to be Madonna. Maybe you don't know who that is, but you probably do. You seem pretty observant.

It'll be nice to meet you soon. I feel like I already know you a little bit. Maybe you feel the same about me.

XOXO, Ashley

I read the note five times. The way I picture Ashley changes with every new letter, but she's always beautiful. She mentioned in her last letter that she wanted a tattoo, so I pictured her with purple hair and five piercings in her ears. Now in my mind she's Madonna with an exotic costume made of colorful leather and a big, blond wig. I'll know for sure who she is when our classes meet in November.

If this were a story, Ashley and I would meet and realize that our eyes are exactly the same color. We would finish each other's sentences and talk about how we've always felt like something was missing. By the end of the story, we would take our DNA to a testing center, and the doctor would tell us that we were long-lost sisters after all. We would get ice cream to celebrate and let it melt all over our fingers while we watched the summer sun set.

I read the letter again and then take out my notebook and pencil to write back to her.

"Hannah, can you come here for a minute?" Mrs. Bloom calls to me from the back of the class. I fold Ashley's letter and put it into my pocket for courage.

"Yes, Mrs. Bloom?" I ask.

"I'm going to have you go and see Ms. Meghan," she says, and writes me a pass. My palms start to perspire.

"Why?"

"It may be helpful to talk to her about that note."

"But we already talked about it in class yesterday."

"I think you could unravel your feelings further with Ms. Meghan."

"I don't feel anything."

Mrs. Bloom leans her head to the side. Her eyes are soft behind her glasses.

"Please go." She hands me the pass, and I take it because I don't want to make a scene.

I walk to Ms. Meghan's office. Her door is open, but I knock anyway. She looks up at me from her desk, dark hair puffed out like it's been through a windstorm. Her face is small and smiley.

"Hi, Hannah. I'm so glad to see you," Ms. Meghan says. She points me toward the circular table and closes the door behind us.

"I'm not upset, Ms. Meghan," I say, just to get things straight.

"Who said you were?" She pours herself a cup of coffee and sits down next to me.

"Isn't that why Mrs. Bloom sent me here?"

"We thought you might like someone to talk to. It must have been upsetting for you to find that note."

"No, it wasn't."

"Are you sure?"

It's starting again. Ms. Meghan has captured me in the clutches of her peach-colored walls and dropped truth serum onto my tongue without me knowing, like the first time I came to her office. That's the only explanation for why I told her about my parents.

If this were a story, I'd write an article for the school newspaper, revealing that Ms. Meghan brews truth serum in her coffeepot. I would have firsthand accounts from other students who had sipped her potion and proceeded to spill their guts, and eyewitnesses who would swear to seeing Ms. Meghan with a suspicious vile of lime-green liquid. If the article ended up on the front page, news channels from all over the country would gather in front of Ms. Meghan's office and demand answers. The chaos would then cause Ms. Meghan's coffeepot to fall onto the floor and crack, leaking truth-fumes through the school and causing everyone to tell their secrets.

But this is clearly not a story, because Brookview doesn't even have a school newspaper.

"Hannah, did you hear me?" Ms. Meghan asks.

"Sorry. I just think maybe the note was a joke," I say.

"What was written on the note?" she asks.

"It said that nobody likes me."

"And that didn't make you sad?"

"No."

"It's okay to tell someone how you feel, Hannah."

*No, it's not.* I mash my lips together so that the words don't come bursting through. I won't let her truth-fumes get me. Two years ago I made a promise not to tell Ms. Meghan anything else. And that promise built an indestructible wall to guard my secrets with. No one can knock it down.

Ms. Meghan leans back in her chair.

"Do you remember that story I told you to read the first time we met?" she asks.

"'Lost in the Funhouse,'" I say, and look at her messy curls. I don't like Ms. Meghan, but I do like the story she gave me.

"Right. Do you remember what you told me about Ambrose after you read the story?"

"Yes. I said that he was too aware of his own thoughts. He couldn't escape them because that's just who he was. Other people could have fun in the funhouse, but not Ambrose. He was different,"

I say. Ms. Meghan nods and smiles slightly.

"You are so smart, Hannah. That story was written for much older people, but you understood how introspective Ambrose was."

"Introspective" means you look at your thoughts and feelings with a magnifying glass, making them larger than life. It makes things harder for people like Ambrose.

"The story is still hard to understand. Even now," I say.

"A lot of stories are. Why don't you look at those passages from 'Lost in the Funhouse' again and let me know what you think this time?"

I would estimate that I have read the passages ninety-six times, but I don't say that.

"Sure."

"How have things been at home? With your parents?" Ms. Meghan asks.

"Great." The word hurts as it escapes.

"Have there been any more fights?"

"Ms. Meghan, can I go? Everything is fine, and I'd really like to get back to class so I can write a letter to my pen pal, Ashley."

Ms. Meghan looks at the clock and pulls her eyebrows together.

"Okay. Come and see me soon," Ms. Meghan says. I close the door behind me and run down the hallway.

I get back to class and start writing my letter to Ashley.

Dear Ashley,
I found a note that said nobody
likes me. I don't want to talk to
anyone about it, just in case it's
true. I would rather not know.
　My stuffed elephant, Ambrose,
came to life last night.
　I'm afraid of a fight every
time I go home.
　Love, Hannah

I tear the note up immediately and stuff it into my desk. I can't tell Ashley any of those things because then she'll be scared of me the way I'm a little scared of me, so I pull out a clean sheet of paper and write my real letter.

Dear Ashley,

I'm so glad you liked the vocabulary list. I don't have time to write one for you now, but I promise I will next time. I haven't thought much about Halloween. You'll make a terrific Madonna. I hope you have fun at your party and that everyone loves your costume.

Meeting you will be my favorite part of the fall. I'm sure of it. Of all the pen pals in the world, you are the most magnificent. I'm sure you know what this word means, but just in case, I'll tell you that it means you are the best one ever.

P.S. Does the middle school have a school newspaper?

Love, Hannah

# Counselor's Notes: Friday, October 9

**Name:** Hannah Geller

**Grade:** Five

**Reason for visit:** Follow-up about a classroom incident involving a hurtful note. This is Hannah's first visit to the office in two years. Previous visit due to unprovoked emotional response and disconcerting comments about home life.

**Demeanor:** Hannah maintained a distant state throughout the visit. Kept arms drawn close to body as if holding self together. She expressed little to no response over the incident, despite the emotional nature. Did not seem especially accepting of visiting the office. This reaction is understandable when considering the parental involvement that resulted from previous visit.

**Visit:** Hannah was not open to discussing the classroom situation. Seemed convinced that there was no real issue behind the note. After conversation about the note, I shifted to home life. She did not offer any information.

**Next action:** Asked Hannah to reread excerpts from a story given during previous session called "Lost in the Funhouse." Story is well above grade level, but Hannah is highly gifted in vocabulary and storytelling. Story was given in an attempt to reveal similarities between herself and perceptive main character, so that she might better understand and ultimately appreciate her introspective nature. Revelation was not fully made in previous sessions. Hoping that another read will accomplish this.

# From Hannah's Pages of "Lost in the Funhouse"

When you're lost, the smartest thing
to do is stay put till you're found. . . .
What's more you might find your own
way yet, *however belatedly.*

# The Fall Festival

Every year at the beginning of October, Brookview holds a fall festival. Popcorn stands and ringtoss games and piles of hay for climbing fill the big open field next to the school. The sky turns lavender, and stars pop into place as I stand in the ticket line with Courtney and Ryan and our parents.

"Guys, I just realized something," Ryan says to Courtney and me. He wears a green glow stick as a necklace.

"What?" we ask.

"This is our last fall festival."

"You're right. Next year we'll be going to a fall dance or something," Courtney gushes. A pink glow stick sits on her head like a fluorescent crown and gives her pale white skin a rosy shine.

"Yuck," Ryan replies while Courtney dances in place. I fidget with my own glow stick, wrapped around my wrist like a handcuff. Ryan looks at me like he knows what I'm thinking. I wouldn't be surprised if one day he confessed that he could read my thoughts like a story, especially the ones when I worry about middle school.

"Our turn," Mom calls from ahead of us. I jog away from Courtney's dance moves and Ryan's knowledgeable eyes.

"Twenty tickets, please," Dad is saying when I wiggle between him and Mom. Mrs. Thyme, my third-grade teacher, is in the booth, dressed like a clown with a round red nose and bushy wig. It's tradition for the teachers to work the fall festival and wear costumes.

My cheeks get warm even though the air is chilly.

"Hi, Hannah. How's fifth grade?" Mrs. Thyme asks. She pulls twenty tickets from a big blue roll, but stares at my blushing face. Her eyes remind me of Ryan's. They know too much.

"It's good," I say, and gather the tickets from her outstretched hand. Dad holds my shoulder and steers me away from the booth. The Grants step up to the window next.

"Did you see the way she looked at us?" Dad asks Mom roughly.

"Come on, Michael. It was nothing," she answers in a hushed voice.

"I'm not looking to be judged at a carnival by a clown."

"Then you shouldn't have given her something to judge."

The Grants finish up at the booth and rejoin us. Mom sticks a smile onto her face. Her bun is pulled back tight tonight, but it took a lot of mousse to make it that way. Dad smiles too, with his hands shoved deep into his pockets. I feel the urge to follow along.

I can't help but think we look like a bunch of clowns with painted-on grins.

When we all have our tickets, Ryan's mom reaches into her purse and hands new glow sticks to Ryan and Courtney and me.

"Last ones. Make them count," she says. Mrs. Grant has long dark hair tied into braids with beads at the ends. The beads tap against each other when she walks. She reminds me of a wind chime, soft and pretty and full of happy sounds.

We hold our blue glow sticks. I don't think you're technically supposed to make wishes on glow sticks, but I take an extra second before I light mine to think about what I would ask for if I could.

If this were a story, genies would live in glow sticks. They would be called Glow Genies and match the color of the tube they came from. When you cracked their home in half, the genies would emerge and tell you to make one wish. Not three, one. I would ask the blue genie for all my family's smiles to be real for the rest of time.

Ryan and Courtney bend their sticks, and color explodes into the tubes. I do the same and watch the blue liquid ignite, but no genie is released. Because this isn't a story.

"The parent-student three-legged race is starting in five minutes." The announcement comes from Principal Jenkins through a megaphone. He wears a scuba diving outfit. It's partly a costume and partly practical, since he spends most of the fall festival as a target in the dunk tank.

Mrs. Grant pulls Ryan into her chest.

"We're doing this, baby. Who's with us?"

I look at Dad, and he takes a hand out of his pocket to give me a thumbs-up. Mr. Gilmore doesn't look so excited but nods at Courtney anyway. Based on what I know about Mr. Gilmore, he probably doesn't want to get his pants dirty. We walk toward the starting line, and I feel lit up like a glow stick, or a full moon. The night is overflowing with the feeling of fall. And fall feels like starting over.

Dad and I tie our legs together with rope and wait for the race to start. Five minutes pass, but no one shouts for us to go. I spot the holdup a few yards away. Mrs. Bloom is there, dressed as a fairy godmother. She holds a piece of rope out to Kimmy Dobson.

"No, it's okay. I don't want to," Kimmy says.

"Are you sure? You were lined up at the starting point. I'd love to race with you."

"I didn't know it was for parents."

"Is your grandma with you?"

"I told you, she's coming. I'm going to meet her right now." Kimmy leaves Mrs. Bloom and the rope behind.

The memory of Kimmy's sympathy card, torn apart and buried in the dirt, fills my mind. I squish a little closer to Dad. I think no matter how loud the sad sounds get, they could never hurt as much as a card full of "I'm sorry you lost your three-legged race partner."

Mrs. Bloom looks at Principal Jenkins, and he lifts his megaphone.

"Ready . . . set . . . go!" he announces. Dad and I take off.

"One, two, one, two," Dad directs. A few other teams get tangled up and trip over themselves. One of those teams is Courtney and Mr. Gilmore.

"Grass stains," they moan together. I almost laugh but am too focused on the finish line. Dad and I keep pace together. One, two, one, two.

Ryan and Mrs. Grant are ahead of us. Mrs. Grant's braids fly out behind her like wings, and Ryan is just plain fast. They cross the finish line a full five seconds before we do.

"Good work, team," Dad says to me, a little out of breath.

We untie ourselves, and Principal Jenkins announces Ryan and his mom as the winners. Their prize is three extra tickets to use on anything at the festival. I get one ticket for coming in second, but I'm just glad that Dad and I finished the race together.

Maybe we could get through whole years just taking things step-by-step. One, two, one, two.

I take the ticket from Principal Jenkins and spot Kimmy in the distance by the exit, alone. I see something else out there with her. A big yellow sign for something that's never been at the fall festival before. A funhouse.

My friends and I and our parents huddle together again. Courtney and Mr. Gilmore brush the dirt off their clothes. Ryan and Mrs. Grant bounce in place like the race has filled them with energy. Dad and I stand quietly and take it all in. It's kind of funny how much we're like our parents.

"Let's go use these tickets," Ryan says. He separates his three prize tickets and gives one each to Courtney and me.

"Where should we go?" Courtney asks.

"This way," I answer, and point toward the funhouse in the back corner.

We tell our parents that we'll meet them in an hour. They go sit at a picnic table with other parents who have probably made the same arrangement with their kids.

"There's no rides back here," Ryan says as we

cross through the fried-food section. The air smells like powdered sugar, but I don't stop to breathe it in. My eyes are fixed on the glowing yellow sign.

"It's not a ride, really. At least I don't think so," I explain.

"Then what is it?"

I stop in front of the funhouse. The front is a long black wall, shaped like a castle. Towers shoot up into the sky, and at the doorway a dragon breathes fire made of ribbons.

"It's a funhouse," I say, although it looks more like a haunted house. I start wondering if I want to go in at all. What if I get lost like Ambrose?

"Uh-oh. Joanie Lawson's in line. Hope she doesn't get too scared, or there will be a mess to clean," Courtney says, loudly enough for some of the other kids around us to giggle into their hands.

Joanie doesn't turn around or say anything back, but I know she heard. She shoves her ticket into the operator's hand (our gym teacher, Mr. West, in a were-wolf costume) and runs into the funhouse.

"What's wrong with you, Court? That was mean as heck," Ryan says.

47

"Oh, please. That's how it works. If it's not some-one else being teased, it could be you. Look what happened with Hannah and that note."

"That's a messed-up way to think. You don't get to put someone down to make yourself feel better." Ryan shakes his head.

I've been friends with Courtney long enough to know that she wasn't always like this. Ryan knows it too. I think if she hadn't been made fun of so much after the *Romeo and Juliet* incident, she wouldn't have the bully bones she does now. I think they grew in right above her rib cage, where they could protect her heart after what happened.

But I swore I'd never talk about *Romeo and Juliet* again, so I won't.

We wait our turn and then give our tickets to Mr. West.

"Welcome to the funhoooouuuse." He howls like a werewolf on the "house" part. It doesn't help me get over the whole haunted house idea. "Have a good time."

My friends and I walk past the fire-breathing dragon and into the funhouse. The first hallway is lit by dim lamps with fake candles inside. Knights in armor line the walls. The wooden door closes behind us, and the room gets darker.

"I don't think I like this," Courtney says.

"Let's keep moving," Ryan suggests.

"We just have to find the right path," I offer.

The deeper we get into the funhouse, the less light there is. There are some small bulbs on the floor, just bright enough for you to see that your legs are still moving, but not enough to show where you are. The glow sticks we're wearing transform from accessories to compasses, guiding us in the dark.

"What's that room? Up ahead?" Ryan asks. I lead us toward an opening at the end of the hallway. We step through the doorway to find a room full of mirrors. There's a foggy, gray lamp on the ceiling casting shadows all over the glass.

Courtney starts laughing.

"Guys, check out the mirrors. We look crazy."

I stand in front of the glass. In one I look like a squished stack of pancakes. In another I'm as tall as a giraffe. In the last one there are a thousand of me staring back, all distorted.

Ryan starts cracking up too. Soon he and Courtney

are bent over from laughing so hard, but all I can do is stare at the mirrors and wonder which Hannah is the real one.

I remember a line from "Lost in the Funhouse."

For whom is the funhouse fun?

Not for Ambrose.

The next group behind us comes into the mirror room, and it gets too crowded, so Ryan and Courtney and I leave, their laughs still bouncing off the walls.

The sun is fully set when we exit the funhouse.

"Good idea, Hannah. That was fun," Ryan says. Courtney nods in agreement.

"It was," I say. Maybe it counts as the truth if it's the way I wish I felt.

We spend the rest of our tickets on salty pretzels and the Ferris wheel and a game where you find the needle in a haystack, but everywhere I look, I see giant dragons and murky mirrors.

Sometimes in stories the ending is left to the reader's interpretation. "Lost in the Funhouse" leaves you wondering if Ambrose ever found his way out. After being in the funhouse myself, I'm wondering if *anyone* ever really does.

# Freak

When I'm back in my room after the fall festival, I pull "Lost in the Funhouse" from the folder it lives in. I don't organize my bookshelf by the author's last name or by color. I group them by theme. I keep Ambrose's story in my Growing Up section with all the Judy Blume books. Those books are old, and they don't use big words, but they teach me about boys and my body. I'm not sure "Lost in the Funhouse" belongs in that section, but I don't have a section for Stories That Know They Are Stories.

"Lost in the Funhouse" isn't a book. It's a collection of photocopied paragraphs that Ms. Meghan picked out for me and then stapled together. I sit on top of my comforter. Ambrose waits on my pillow. I take a breath and blow out magic, releasing the worry that Ambrose won't talk to me again, that it was just in my head the whole time.

Ambrose makes a sound like an elephant yawn.

"Good night, Ambrose," I say with a heart full of relief.

"Good night?" he answers.

"I wasn't sure what to say. It's nighttime now. The moon is out."

"The moon is always out."

Ambrose talks like "Lost in the Funhouse," in sentences that sound like bits of a poem. By this point you probably think this is a story, because my stuffed elephant is still talking to me and that seems impossible. But I promise, he really is.

"Tell me again, Ambrose. Why have you never woken up before?" I ask.

"You haven't needed me."

I stick out my lip and cross my arms.

"That's not true. I've always needed you."

"I'm sorry. I'm here now."

I put Ambrose in between my legs and hold the pages out in front of us. I start to read aloud to him. By the time I get to the middle of the pages, I'm crying into Ambrose's gray skin.

If this were a story, a musician would be sitting on a stool in the corner of my room, playing an acoustic

guitar. He would bring his face close to the microphone and say, "This one's for you, Hannah." When
the lyrics started, my heart would feel like breaking
because they were written too perfectly, written just
for me.

This is how "Lost in the Funhouse" makes me
feel.

# As Told by Ambrose

"That no one chose what he was was unbearable," Hannah reads from the story in front of her.

Hannah's tears feel like raindrops. I know what raindrops feel like, because she left me outside in a summer storm once.

"What's wrong?" I ask, but I already know. I know everything about Hannah.

"Either everyone has felt what Ambrose feels, in which case it goes without saying, or no normal person feels such things, in which case Ambrose is a freak."

She is not talking about me. She means Ambrose from the story, the one who got himself lost in his own thoughts. I can see that Hannah is doing the same thing now.

"Hannah?"

"I'm a freak, Ambrose. I'm not normal. I don't want to be this way." The words tumble out of her mouth.

The solution is simple, but I can tell she is not ready to hear it. I try anyway.

"So stop keeping all your feelings inside you," I reply.

"I don't know what else to do with them."

She tosses the pages to the ground and lies on her side, knees tucked up to her chest. I want to smooth out her dark hair and wipe the wetness from her powder-blue eyes, but that is not how this works.

"You'll figure it out."

"Don't leave me," she says.

"I couldn't if I wanted to."

She holds my stuffed arm and closes her eyes. I watch her fall asleep. I live only because of Hannah. I live only because of all the wonder she has inside her. She does not even know what she's capable of.

# Penny

On Sunday, I go grocery shopping with Mom, and Courtney comes with us. She lives in a big house on top of a hill. The grass looks fresh and green even though it's October and wet leaves should have turned the yard to mud. It's like Courtney still lives in summertime.

Courtney bounces down her front steps, and Mrs. Gilmore watches through the screen door. She waves to Mom, and Mom waves back. Mom is just as beautiful as Mrs. Gilmore, but Mom looks much more tired. Sometimes I wonder how many hours of sleep she would need to not be so tired anymore, but something tells me there's no answer.

"Hi, Mrs. Geller," Courtney says politely when she gets into the car. Mom smiles into the rearview mirror and backs out of the Gilmores' twisty driveway.

"How much money do you have?" I whisper to Courtney.

"Ten dollars," she whispers back, and pulls the bill from her big pink purse.

Courtney is supposed to spend the money on fruit cups or veggie sticks or yogurt with granola packaged in the lid, but we have our own plans.

"What are you two whispering about back there?" Mom asks.

"Nothing," I say. Courtney seals her mouth with an invisible key.

Sometimes I wish it weren't so easy to lie.

Mom lets us go off on our own when we get to ShopRite. We wait for her to disappear down an aisle before we take off across the store. I hear Courtney laughing behind me and see the bank next to the bakery, which smells like fresh doughnuts. All of my senses are occupied by happy feelings. There's no room for bad things to touch me.

We stop in front of the bank, and Courtney takes out her ten-dollar bill. We face each other and hold hands. Our arms make a loop that never ends.

"Ready?" Courtney asks.

"Ready," I say.

The lady at the bank counter watches us approach. Her face tells us that whatever our question is, the answer is no. But we are on a mission. Courtney puts her money on the counter, and we stand elbow to elbow.

"I would like twenty rolls of pennies for this, please," Courtney says with her high-pitched-honey-sweet adult voice.

"Where are your parents?" the lady asks.

"We are old enough to make this transaction without them, ma'am, but thank you for your concern," I say. Bank Lady is not amused. If this were a story, Bank Lady would reveal herself to be a robot and shoot laser beams out of her eyes. She would chase us through the aisles, and we'd do backflips to avoid her until her robot batteries died.

"What could you need all those pennies for?"

"We're coin collectors," Courtney says. Finally the cold look on Robot Bank Lady's face transforms to sunshine.

"I collect stamps," she says, and takes our ten-dollar bill to the back room. She returns with our rolls of pennies in a plastic bag.

"Thank you," we both say, and gather up the rolls. She smiles at us. I hope that one day she finds the rarest stamp in her robot galaxy and her collection is complete.

The truth is, we're not coin collectors. We're secret coin droppers. Courtney reaches into the plastic bag and hands me a roll. I tear the paper and catch a glimpse of the shiny copper, like a golden ticket in a Wonka Bar. My brain spins like a pinwheel, and before I can stop it, I am thinking about Violet Beauregarde and how scared she must have been when she thought she was going to explode. I think about Mike Teevee being shrunk so small that he almost didn't exist anymore. I think about how their day at the chocolate factory was ruined because they were who they were. *It's just a story, it's just a story. That's what characters do. They teach us a lesson.*

"Anyone in there?" Courtney's voice stops the turning pages in my head. She taps on my temple with her knuckles.

"I'm here. Let's do this," I say, and pull a penny from the roll.

The rules of coin dropping are simple. Always leave the penny faceup. And don't let anyone see you do it, or else the penny loses its luck. Courtney and I creep down the aisles, looking for good spots. The cereal aisle is empty. We nod to each other and leave our faceup pennies on the tile floor. Two down. We won't make it through all the rolls, but it feels nice to have one thousand chances to make someone happy.

"You take frozen foods. I'm going to the fruit," Courtney says, and we part ways. I don't like when Courtney and I separate, because it feels like I'm bothering her. Losing her. Like she's been drowning in our friendship and needs to come up for air.

I wonder if she liked me more when we were five and I didn't know so many words yet and my skin didn't have mountain ranges made of red pimples. I squeeze the roll of pennies and walk down the frosty frozen food aisle, remembering that it's just me and Courtney on this secret mission. That means even when we separate, we're still in this together. I pull out a new penny and inspect it, running my finger over its ridges.

"Where should I put you?" I ask absentmindedly.

"Don't leave me here!" the penny yells. I almost

drop it, but manage to hold on. If it had landed face-down, who knows what could have happened.

I look around. There's a woman in high heels contemplating ice cream, and an old man on a scooter filling his basket with frozen lima beans. I make sure they aren't watching me and hold the penny to my face.

"How are you talking to me?" I ask.

"You!" the penny yells. I wish the penny would quiet down, but no one else seems to notice her, or the magic bursting from my heart like a shooting star.

I know what you're thinking. The penny is coming to life now? This is definitely a story. But the penny is really talking to me! And loudly too, like she's trying to make herself seem bigger than she is. Bigger than one cent.

"I brought you to life just like I did with Ambrose?"

"Yes! I'm Penny!"

"Nice to meet you, Penny. Can I ask you something? Ambrose lets me ask him things."

"Yes!"

"Does Courtney really want to be my friend?" I ask.

"I'm cold!" Penny says.

I sigh. My magic might give objects a voice, but it sure doesn't keep them from getting off topic like a scatterbrained protagonist in a story.

"Okay, I'll leave you somewhere else."

"Clean up, aisle seven!" Penny screams.

"You're funny," I say, and take Penny to aisle seven. She sings an Oompa-Loompa song while we walk.

"How do you know Willy Wonka, Penny?"

"I saw the movie!"

I laugh out loud at the thought of Penny with an oversize bucket of popcorn, taking up a whole seat in a dark movie theater. Part of me wants to keep Penny in my pocket, but that's not her purpose. She was made for someone else to find. There's no one in the aisle, so I bend down and let Penny go.

"Good-bye, and good luck," I say.

"What are you doing?" a voice sneers from behind me. I know right away it's not Penny. I stand up and twirl around. Kimmy Dobson is there in a green checkered shirt. Her oily skin gleams in the grocery store lighting. She looks at me like I've just beaten her in the spelling bee again. Kimmy might be a super-skilled wordsmith, but she's never won the spelling bee, and I'm the reason why.

Last year's bee was soon after Kimmy's mom died. I remember when it was over, she snuck up behind me and whispered, "I bet you've never lost anything in your life." Her breath felt like angry wildfire in my ear. I couldn't tell whether she was talking about spelling bees or parents, but I felt those burning words on my skin for a long time after she walked away.

"I'm not doing anything," I say, and turn away from her. Kimmy grips my shoulder and pulls.

"I see all those pennies in your hand. Are you seriously just throwing them away? Some people actually need money, you know."

"They're lucky pennies," I say, sounding dumb. I wonder if Courtney and I have made a mistake. I look at Penny, alone and abandoned on the ground, all her luck drained away because Kimmy saw me drop her. Maybe Penny would've been better off in a register.

"Pennies are money, *Han*-nah, not a good-luck charm. No wonder no one likes you," Kimmy barks.

Her words feel heavy, like the rolls of pennies in my hand.

"How did you know what the note said?"

"What are you talking about? Just hand over the pennies."

I hold out the rest of the rolls, because I don't know what else to do. See, now you know this isn't a story, because if it were, I'd be tough enough to stand up to the bully. Or brave enough to tell her that she didn't need to be so mean, even if she lost her mom.

"Don't give those to her," Courtney chimes in. She comes up behind me and closes my hand with hers.

"Of course little rich girl throws the pennies away too. Does your mansion have a garbage can just for coins?" Kimmy asks.

"Does your trailer park have a rule against soap?" Courtney snaps back.

Kimmy takes a step closer to us. She towers over Courtney, but my best friend doesn't budge.

"Hand them over," Kimmy says.

"Okay."

Courtney takes a penny from a roll and whips it at

Kimmy. It hits her in the shoulder and bounces to the ground. Before Kimmy can react, Courtney throws another and another. She turns to me.

"Come on, Hannah. Help me," she says.

I don't want to help, but Kimmy has left a coin-shaped hole in my chest. I take a penny and throw it.

"Weeee," the penny cries as it flies into Kimmy's forehead.

"You're going to regret this," Kimmy says, and turns her back on us.

"Good work, team." Courtney gives me a high five. I should feel better, but instead I feel slimy.

*Did the person who wrote the note feel better when they dropped it onto the floor? If I wrote a note back to them, would that make me a bully too?*

*How did Kimmy know that the note said no one likes me?*

"Maybe that was a bad idea," I say.

"Are you saying that she gets to be awful to everyone but no one gets to be awful to her?"

"Well . . ."

"She's all talk and smell, Hannah. We won."

If this were a story, an X-ray machine would show

that Courtney's bully bones are stronger than all the others. The doctor would diagnose her with *Romeo and Juliet* disease and write on a prescription pad that everyone around her should just wait until that day doesn't haunt her anymore. No matter how hard it gets.

I see Mom turn the corner into our aisle. She waves us over. The cart is full of Dad's favorite soda and my favorite apple cinnamon oatmeal. I think about how Mom has no favorites. There is nothing in the cart just for her.

"Ready to go, girls?" she asks. Courtney stuffs our rolls of pennies into her pink purse. We'll save them for next time.

When I turn back to look at Penny one more time, I see that she's disappeared. Someone must have picked her up.

"Bye, Penny," I whisper to the empty aisle.

We see Kimmy again on our way out through the automatic doors. She sits alone on a bench outside the store with a spelling book in her hands.

Maybe Violet Beauregarde had a hard time at school. Maybe Mike Teevee's dad was never home.

We only see what people want us to see. We are all unreliable narrators.

Mom's phone rings through the car speakers on the way home. She clicks a button on the dashboard and starts to say hello.

"Where are you?" Dad's loud voice fills up the car. Mom rushes to take the call off the speakers and puts the phone to her ear, even though that's illegal. I squeeze the strap of my seat belt, and my brain fills with permutations of what will happen when we get home. The word "permutations" is usually used for math problems but can be used for Dad problems too.

"What happened?" Mom says softly into the phone. A moment later she says, "Hello?"

Dad must not have answered. She hangs up.

"We're going to take you home, Courtney, okay?" Mom says.

"But she was supposed to stay for dinner," I argue.

"Not now." Mom tugs on her seat belt like it's strangling her.

"Okay, Mrs. Geller," Courtney replies.

Courtney stares at me from the other bucket seat,

but I don't turn my head from the window, even when she gets out of the car. The last drops of sun fall behind the orange trees as we drive home. Mom forgets to put the radio back on, so the car is too quiet, a sad-day sound with no sound at all. Her bun is falling apart. We pull into the driveway, and I pray to find Dad in his recliner with a Coke watching a football game where the Packers are winning by one hundred points.

"Get the bags," Mom says, and rushes into the house.

I walk to the trunk of the car and load up my arms with plastic bags, before following behind.

"Can't find a thing in this house. It's a mess, always," Dad yells when I open the door. I gently place the bags on the counter and glance into the living room. There's an empty box for a big-screen TV on the floor and parts lying all over. Dad is kneeling behind the stand with the new TV on it. He has a flashlight in his hand. His face is Coke-can red.

"What were you looking for?" Mom asks.

"Everything! Wrench, batteries . . ." I walk back to the car to pick up more groceries. I gather slivers of the fight each time I go back and forth. In and out.

"... out for hours ...," Dad says.

"... shopping for food ...," Mom says.

"... sick of not being able to do one thing."

"... not my fault."

There are no more bags. I put away the groceries and try to find a story in the boxes of spaghetti or the frozen pizza, but can't come up with anything. I walk to the little desk in the kitchen and quietly open the junk drawer. The pack of batteries peaks out from underneath the roll of postage stamps and some pencils. I pull a few batteries from the pack.

"Here, Dad," I offer, and hold them out. Maybe if I can give him what he's looking for, the gathering fight will clear, like a cloud that decides not to rain and lets sunlight through instead. The sound of my heartbeat roars in my ears, and the batteries shake in my hand.

Dad doesn't listen. He keeps grunting behind the TV stand. It wobbles and wobbles, and before anyone can stop it, the TV falls from the stand. The sound it makes against the hardwood floor is loud and permanent. Dad swears and leans the TV back upright.

One single crack cuts across the screen from corner to corner like a fault line, a place where the earth splits in half like a broken heart.

I wish I were in a story. Then I could rewrite things to end the way I want them to and erase all the bad parts.

I run upstairs. My door can't seal out the screaming. I put my head under my comforter. There's a feeling in my chest like a leaky sailboat, and I would give anything, anything, anything to make the sinking stop.

# From Hannah's Pages of "Lost in the Funhouse"

In a perfect funhouse you'd be able to go only one way . . . getting lost would be impossible.

# Date Stamps

The two fifth-grade classes meet in the library for the preliminary spelling bee.

"'Monumental.' *M-o-n-u-m-e-n-t-a-l*," I say to the librarian, Mrs. Raymond, our moderator.

"Congratulations, Hannah. You'll be our last finalist." The fifth-grade classes clap for me. Kimmy, another finalist, crosses her arms like a defense against more flying pennies.

I manage a weak smile about the victory, but yesterday is still taking up all the space inside my head. It's hard to notice the thick library carpet under my feet or the smell of books in the air when last night's fight is like a song left on repeat. I'm still watching it like a movie on a cracked TV screen.

*"Maybe it's time,"* Dad yelled.

*"I couldn't agree more,"* Mom answered.

I shake my head hard to make the memories go quiet. Courtney and Ryan stand in front of me, watching.

"Surprise, you won a spelling bee," Courtney says.

"I almost messed up 'artificial.'"

"But you didn't." Ryan pulls from his back pocket a looped piece of yarn with a soda can tab attached, and drapes it around my neck. "Your medal."

"Ryan, you were supposed to find a gold tab." Courtney puts her hands on her hips.

"It's okay. I love it." I grip the makeshift medal so tight, it leaves a mark in the shape of a figure eight.

"Was everything okay last night?" Courtney asks.

The medal starts to feel hot in my hand.

"What do you mean?"

"You know, with your parents. Your mom wouldn't let me come over."

Ryan looks at me. I hope there aren't secrets on my face like swollen zits.

"I'll tell you later. We only have a few minutes to get books."

I turn away from my friends and head for the fiction section. I run my hand over the laminated book bindings and pretend not to see Courtney and Ryan whispering where I left them. Being close to the books quiets my mind for a second. I pull one from the shelf and open to the very back.

My favorite part of a library book is the card with the date stamps in the back that tell you when the book is due. Some libraries don't use them anymore, but ours still does. I like the way the due dates stack up on top of each other in different colors of ink. I like the feeling that no matter what year it is or whatever else changes, this book will always be the same. The world will keep turning as long as this story exists.

"Time's up," Mrs. Bloom announces. I close the book and quickly check it out at the counter. Mrs. Raymond stamps the due date, November 6, into the back with blue ink. I hug the book to my chest and take in a huge lungful of library book air when we line up at the door.

Kimmy pushes Courtney aside to stand behind me. She smells like wet dirt.

"I'll end this when we get to the finals," Kimmy whispers into my ear.

*Maybe it's time.*

I squeeze my eyes shut until the voices from the

past and the present stop colliding like a car crash that I can't make sense of.

Later my class grabs our lunches from the shelves. My area is next to Courtney's—Geller beside Gilmore, like always. I see her bend down to pick something up near her backpack. A scrunched-up piece of white paper. Before I can say a word, she opens the note. Her eyes follow whatever is written on the paper, and then spring up to my face.

"Hannah?" she says.

"What's wrong?" I ask.

She hands me the note with a look like she wishes her last name was Zoo, so she could be miles of cubbies away from me. I don't know what's worse, that look or the note.

WHY WOULD ANYONE BE FRIENDS WITH HANNAH?

# As Told by Ambrose

Ambrose?" Hannah asks.

"Hannah," I answer. She lets out a heavy sigh. I know she still thinks I'll leave at any minute.

She looks to her bedspread. Her skin is as white as a paper ghost. Black hair hides her face like a shield made of velvet.

"There was another note today." Hannah pulls me into her chest, where I can't see her eyes.

"What's going to happen?"

Hannah pauses before she answers.

"I can feel the notes hurting me, Ambrose. I know I want them to stop. But is it weird to think that they might help?"

"How could they possibly help?" I wonder.

"People are starting to see me."

"People already see you, Hannah. Lots of people."

Hannah puts me back down on the bed and goes to sit at her desk. I watch her stare out the foggy window.

It's hard to see Hannah observe her memories until they turn into a scary movie. Not even I can turn it off.

I've heard the fights too. The voices slip into Hannah's bedroom like a thief in the middle of the night. I've seen Hannah sit with her ear to the door and wait for them to pass. I've seen her run to hide her head under the pillow. The fights dig holes in her mind, I know it, but she won't tell anyone how to fill them back up.

The first time she brought me downstairs with her, the heaviness in that room almost crushed me.

# Sneakers

The next day Mrs. Bloom writes up a bulletin and tells us to give it to our parents. It invites them to the meeting we are having tomorrow with Ms. Meghan about the notes. I fold the bulletin, and the edge slips across my finger. A cut appears and turns red. Maybe paper cuts hurt as much as being run over by a minivan. Pain is pain.

Before recess we have time to read new letters from our pen pals and respond. When I hold Ashley's letter, my heart becomes an overstuffed envelope, all full of excitement on the inside but calm and collected on the outside. I tear open the seal and read.

Dear Hannah,

I like your random questions. They make me feel useful somehow, ha-ha. There's no school newspaper here at the middle school. I'm not sure anyone would read it if there was. Everyone's kind of in their own world. We could probably all write our own newspapers about ourselves, fill it up with news and gossip and advice columns. Mine would be called The Ashley Report. What would you call yours?

See you in a few weeks!

XOXO, Ashley

In my head Ashley becomes a newspaper reporter with a pencil tucked behind her ear and ink stains on her fingers and the prettiest smile the world has ever seen. I take out a clean sheet of paper and write a new letter.

Dear Ashley,

I shouldn't be telling you this, but I drop heads-up pennies all over town. Well, the parts of town I can get to. If you've ever looked down at the ground and found a lucky penny, it's possible that I'm the one who put it there. I like the thought of that. It's like in some way we've already met.

I have another random question for you. I hope it makes you feel useful. What do you think is the purpose of a penny? Is it to be something magical, or something practical? I'm just wondering whether you would rather find a heads-up penny and keep it for luck, or use it to buy a slurpee if the total comes to $1.01.

Maybe you can answer this question for me when I visit you at the middle school. Maybe it's a stupid question, but I like to think that you would understand.

P.S. My newspaper would be called Story Time.

Love, Hannah

When we've all put our letters into envelopes, Mrs. Bloom lets us go outside. I walk to the swings where Courtney and Ryan and I usually meet up, but

Courtney doesn't follow me. She goes to sit on the hill with Rebecca, who wears flower crowns and owns forty-six lip glosses. It's like the words on the note have really made Courtney wonder why she should be friends with me.

The October air feels more like December air today—but the December air after the holidays, when the world seems a little deflated, when the lights on the houses shine less than they did before.

I am relieved when Ryan's class rushes out the door and he comes over to the swings.

"Where's Courtney?" he asks. I point to the hill. Rebecca is braiding Courtney's hair. Ryan sits next to me on the swing and starts pumping his legs. I see that his sneakers are falling apart.

"So there was another note," Ryan says. It's a statement, not a question.

"Yeah." I kick at the wood chips on the ground.

"What did it say?"

I start to swing with him. I understand words, but I don't understand how two swings moving back and forth together will eventually fall out of sync. The physics of things confuses me.

"Why would anyone be friends with Hannah?"

Ryan drags his heels across the rubber mat to slow down. He grabs the chain on my swing, and I come to a stop.

"I'm gonna find out who wrote that note and tell them a thousand reasons why I'm friends with you."

"You don't have to worry about me, Ry."

He keeps holding tight to my swing and lowers his brown eyes to the ground. They look a little stormy.

"My parents both lost their teaching jobs before school started," he says. I blink at him, unsure what to say.

"I'm sorry. I didn't know."

"It was hard for me to tell anyone. Even you and Court. But we have to be there for each other. If you're feeling bad about these notes, you should talk about it," he says.

Ryan smiles. His skin is a shade that reminds me of autumn, a brown that shines brightly. I wonder why people notice the difference between Ryan's skin and mine, when he always makes me feel better in my own. Pimples and all.

"Tomorrow we'll fix your shoes. I still have rolls left from our duct tape phase," I say.

"You have that roll with the lightning bolts?"

"Yup."

"Awesome."

I want to tell Ryan about the fighting, about Ambrose and Penny, about the way my mind won't turn off, but it's easier to store words up like emergency supplies than open my mouth and use them.

"Mind if I swing alone for a while?" I ask.

Ryan shakes his head and then runs on his broken sneakers to play kickball with the other boys. I push myself off the ground and start to swing. Back and forth, back and forth. I tilt my head back to face the blue sky. If anyone could know who wrote the notes, it would be the sky. It must see everything.

"Who did it?" I whisper.

I find the sky's voice in the breeze, light and wispy. It calls out each time I swing.

"They." *Forward.* "Did." *Back.*

I look around. The entire fifth grade is out on the playground. A whole bunch of possible *theys.*

"Can't you give me a hint?"

"They're." *Forward.* "On." *Back.* "The." *Forward.* The sky is cut off by the sound of a whistle. Recess is over.

On the hill? On the parallel bars? On the sun?

I go to meet my class in line. I'll have to solve the mystery without help from the sky.

# Roller Coaster

My parents drive me to school on the day of the class meeting about the notes. Dad's at the wheel and has his hand on Mom's knee. Mom is quiet beside him. They haven't been fighting as much since I handed them Mrs. Bloom's bulletin.

"What will the counselor be saying to the class?" Dad asks.

"I don't know," I say.

"You don't seem very concerned, Hannah. One of your classmates is bullying you."

I don't want to be concerned about the notes, so I think about a part of "Lost in the Funhouse" that scared me. Ambrose recounts the night that a roller coaster flew off the tracks and onto the boardwalk. Those things aren't supposed to happen, but they do.

Thinking about it reminds me of this past summer when Courtney's parents took us to the amusement park. It was around the same time that rose-colored zits were springing up on my face. Courtney and I were by the soda fountain, filling paper cups with free drinks.

"Dark soda causes breakouts," Courtney said. I poured my cola down the drain and refilled with lemon-lime, clear and bubbly.

Courtney wanted to ride the roller coaster. I followed behind with my head bowed away from the hot sun, because sweat causes breakouts too. We lined up outside the ride. There was a sign hanging on the white fence. Pregnant women should not ride; people with heart conditions should not ride. I thought, who doesn't have a problem with their heart?

"You should tell your mom to buy you foundation," Courtney said.

"Why?" I asked.

"The best way to handle your problem is to cover it up."

I didn't feel old enough to have this problem surfacing on my skin or to go on the upside-down roller coaster. When we got to the front of the line, a ride attendant carried a measuring stick and walked along the row of riders. He held the stick out toward me, nodded, and walked away.

*Can't you see?* I wanted to ask. *I'm not tall enough to ride.*

When the ride was over, I got out of the cart, walked to the bathroom, and quietly threw up. I had nightmares for a week that I was on the roller coaster from "Lost in the Funhouse," sailing through the stars into nothingness.

I wonder if this is the type of memory Ms. Meghan wanted to loosen from my brain when she told me to reread Ambrose's story. I put a hand to my bumpy cheek and hope that whenever I meet with her again, she won't ask me about the part with the roller coaster.

"I am worried, Dad," I say.

He smiles reassuringly at me in the rearview mirror. Stress causes breakouts.

# The Pledge

My class sits in a half circle on the carpet, with our parents in chairs behind us. Ms. Meghan sits in her own chair in front of us. She has tried to tame her hair into a ponytail, but the curls still stick out in all directions.

"Who here has ever been bullied?" she asks.

Almost everyone in my class raises their hand a little. I forget to raise mine. My dad nudges me, and I quickly lift my arm.

"How did that make you feel?"

"Scared," Rebecca offers.

"Sad," Courtney says. I watch Courtney's mom run her fingers through Courtney's hair.

"Like I wanted to fight back," Kimmy says, and she looks at me when she says it. She has no parents sitting in a plastic chair behind her.

"Scared, sad, angry. All those emotions can arise when a person feels singled out. And when those feelings do happen, it can be very hard to make them go away. Like when you drop a glass onto the floor. It's hard to reassemble those pieces to fit just right again, isn't it?"

The class nods.

"Does anyone have any questions?"

"Is someone going to get in trouble for the notes?" Kimmy asks. Everyone looks at Ms. Meghan like they were all wondering the same thing. Ms. Meghan's mouth goes up in a half smile that seems disappointed.

"We're not meeting today to talk about a punishment. I'm here to ask that the bullying in this class stop. You're all fifth graders now. That means you are role models for the younger students at Brookview. This time of your life is a big deal. You're almost in middle school. Not a single one of you should be hurting because of bullying." Ms. Meghan's eyes scan our half circle. I look away when she gets to me, then remember that looking away implies I have something to hide. I lift my head back up, but she has already moved on.

"Today we're going to sign a pledge." She reaches into the bag she brought with her. There are cows printed on the outside. She pulls out a set of paints and a rolled-up piece of paper.

"We pledge to treat one another with respect," Ms. Meghan reads from the paper, "and speak to one another with kind words. We pledge to stop bullying when we see it. We will use all of our knowledge, heart, and strength to make our school a safe and happy place for everyone." She lays the paper on the floor in front of us.

"You'll sign this pledge with a painted handprint. Come pick your colors."

My classmates crawl across the floor to grab a paint bottle and brush.

"That's it? Finger painting?" Dad chimes in from behind me.

"Sir?" Ms. Meghan replies.

"My daughter is being targeted."

"We are going to figure out what happened. Hannah, is there anything you would like to say?"

Everyone stops painting to look at me.

Dad puts a hand on my shoulder. My cheeks turn hot like they're being toasted.

"I feel like I'm in a story," I say.

Kimmy laughs, until Mrs. Bloom glances over from her desk.

"You're right. These things can seem a little unreal," Ms. Meghan says. I move away from Dad and pick a purple paint bottle, so that everyone knows I'm done talking.

When we finish signing our pledge, Mrs. Bloom dismisses the parents. They stand up from their too-small chairs. Dad squeezes my shoulder and whispers that he'll see me at home. Mom gives me a hug and tells me to have a good day, and then she follows him.

Our pledge is hung on the back wall. I have been trying not to think about the person behind the pencil, but now all our handprints are on a piece of paper, and it's hard not to realize that one of those hands wrote the notes.

# Counselor's Notes:
## Thursday, October 15

**Name:** Ryan Grant

**Grade:** Five

**Reason for visit:** Ryan came on his own to discuss his concerns about a friend.

**Demeanor:** Ryan maintains a smile throughout visit, even when discussing his thoughts about his friend. Starts the visit by making friendly small talk. He is a serious delight.

**Visit:** Transcript is as follows:

COUNSELOR: You're here to talk about Hannah?

STUDENT: I'm worried about her. About the notes.

COUNSELOR: What's worrying you the most?

STUDENT: Well, she won't talk about it. She won't talk about anything. Ever. She just keeps saying she's fine.

COUNSELOR: What do you think is holding her back?

STUDENT: I don't know. We've been friends since kindergarten, but she still doesn't trust me.

COUNSELOR: This might not be about trust. This is an obstacle that Hannah has to overcome within herself.

STUDENT: But I'm her friend. I want to help her.

COUNSELOR: I'm sure you help her more than you know.

STUDENT: There's nothing I can do, then?

COUNSELOR: Just keep being there.

**Next action:** Make this student president of the United States.

# Suspects

If this were a story, my class would become suspects in a lineup behind glass. They would wait to be identified as the perpetrator. No one would be ruled out, not even Mrs. Bloom. The other side of the glass would be invisible to them, so they couldn't see me with the police and lawyers and school principal, trying to decide who was guilty.

I sit at my desk and take the investigation into my own hands. While everyone else works on math problems, I start collecting clues. Rebecca walks to the back of the class to sharpen her pencil.

*Reasons it might be Rebecca Snow: The note was found by the pencil sharpener. She sharpens her pencil at least ten times a day, due to status as overachieving note taker.*

Rebecca walks back to her desk and starts writing again, using every inch of the paper. I cross her name off the list. She would never waste valuable space by ripping corners out of her notebook.

The lines on my paper fill with detective notes.

*Reasons it might be Theo Baywood:*
*He told me he liked me in*
*fourth grade, and I ran away.*


*Reasons it might be Joanie Lawson:*
*I didn't stop Courtney from*
*teasing her when Joanie peed her*
*pants during a scary movie.*

It might be Courtney, because she has hardly spoken to me since the day the note asked her why anyone would be friends with me.

I close my notebook. It's too gloomy to think about the reasons why someone wouldn't like me. Maybe I've done some things I shouldn't, but I hoped that people would be able to see past my mistakes.

My life is becoming a one-way police mirror. As hard as I try to see what lies ahead, the glass stays dark. All I can see is my shadowy reflection.

# Caterpillar Tables

The tables in the cafeteria look like colorful caterpillars, long and broken into segments. The segments separate one group of friends from another. If this were a story, the tables would turn into butterflies when people defaced them with swear words and stained them with pizza sauce. All of the damage would turn into beautiful designs on their wings, and one day they would fly away through the cafeteria's emergency exit. We'd all be left in awe and with nowhere to sit.

Courtney, Ryan, and I always sit on the far end of the blue caterpillar (I mean "table") at the back of the cafeteria, in front of the stage. On the Monday after making our pledge to Ms. Meghan, Courtney walks into the cafeteria with Rebecca and her friends. They all have blond hair and clear skin. They head toward the green caterpillar (I mean "table") in the middle of the room.

"Court!" Ryan calls out from our corner. Courtney

rolls her eyes. She says something to her new blond friends and comes over to us.

"I'm sitting with Rebecca today. You can come if you want, Ryan," she says. Ryan looks back and forth between the two of us.

"Why can't Hannah come?" he asks.

"No room," Courtney says. I turn in my seat to look at her.

"Are we not friends anymore?" I ask. Courtney throws her hands up. It almost feels like déjà vu, because Courtney has stopped being my friend so many times in my head.

"Stop being dramatic. Are you coming, Ryan?"

Ryan tilts his head at me, and then picks up his meatball grinder.

"I'm okay here," he says, and digs in.

Courtney walks away, and my heart fills with holes like a caterpillar-bitten leaf. I never thought her footsteps would be a sad-day sound.

# From Hannah's Pages of "Lost in the Funhouse"

In the fun-house mirror-room you can't see yourself go on forever, because no matter how you stand, your head gets in the way.

# Hang in There

A week passes. No one comes forward to say they wrote the notes. Mrs. Bloom gives us new letters from our pen pals. I feel better when I hold the envelope.

Dear Hannah,

Are you okay, girl? You seem a little down lately. I realize that a letter is not the best way to ask someone if they're doing all right. Things can change a lot day to day.

 To answer your question, I'd probably go with the magic penny. I don't really like Slurpees.

 Hang in there, girl. I'll be seeing you soon.

 XOXO, Ashley

Ashley transforms in my head again. Now she looks like a 1970s schoolgirl from the pictures in our history books, or from Mom's old photo albums. I imagine Ashley with sandy brown hair and wire-rim glasses and a schoolgirl skirt. She carries books tucked under her arm. In her bedroom she has a lava lamp and that popular poster of a kitten dangling from a branch saying, HANG IN THERE.

Dear Ashley,
Of course I'm okay, because you like magic pennies too. I'll add that to the list of reasons why you're my favorite pen pal.
Love, Hannah.

# Human Knot

In gym class a few days before Halloween, Mr. West splits us up into groups and tells the members of each group to stand in a circle. I'm with Courtney, Kimmy, Rebecca, and three boys. Mr. West tells us to cross our arms and hold hands with two other people in the circle.

I reach for Courtney, but she shifts and reaches for Rebecca. I end up holding the slippery hand of one boy, and the other goes to Kimmy. She squeezes harder than she needs to, and I want to cry. Our tangled arms form a human knot.

"This is the Halloween Spiderweb Game. Work together to free yourselves without letting go of your classmates' hands," Mr. West says, and blows his whistle. His whistle is almost always in his mouth. He blows it no matter what game we're playing. I think he would blow it even if we were playing the Quiet Game.

My group starts squirming around without a

plan. The boys hurtle over our arms and twist us into an even bigger mess.

"Guuuys, you're pulling me," Rebecca says.

"Stop whining," Kimmy snaps back.

I'm quiet while I stare at our knot of limbs. It looks like an unsolvable problem. I start to panic. I wonder if we will be stuck like this forever. I wonder if I will ever be able to clean up the mess that the notes left behind, if Courtney will ever speak to me again now that everything has gotten so twisted. My lungs feel full of water, and I can't breathe. I let go of the hands that keep me fastened to the human knot and backpedal out of the circle.

"You're not supposed to do that, Hannah," Rebecca says. Courtney glares.

"I'm sorry," I say.

"Those notes were right," Kimmy mumbles under her breath.

That's it. The answer. The way to fix things.

If this were a story, then this part would be called the turning point, the moment when new information is revealed and some of the pieces fall into place, like a half-finished puzzle.

"I'm sorry," I say again. I run to Mr. West and ask him if I can go see Ms. Meghan. He says through his whistle that I can.

Ms. Meghan's door is open. Her wild hair seems to expand even farther when she sees me.

"Hannah, please, come in," she says. I come inside but don't sit in the chair.

"I know who did it. I know who wrote the notes," I say. She tries to get me to sit down, but I won't. I want this to be over. I want to be free of the knot.

"Who did it?" Ms. Meghan asks.

"It was Kimmy. Kimmy Dobson wrote them."

# Counselor's Notes:
# Tuesday, October 27

**Name:** Hannah Geller

**Grade:** Five

**Reason for visit:** Hannah came to office to suggest who was responsible for the bullying notes.

**Demeanor:** She seemed relieved to name fellow classmate as potential offender. Was passionate in her belief that the information was true. Came into office without hesitation.

**Visit:** Transcript follows.

> COUNSELOR: Hannah, why do you believe Kimmy did this?
>
> STUDENT: Everything I do makes her mad.
>
> COUNSELOR: Have you considered that Kimmy might have other things upsetting her?
>
> STUDENT: I beat her in the spelling bee every year, and she thinks that I throw away money.
>
> COUNSELOR: Do you throw away money?

STUDENT: I don't see it that way.

COUNSELOR: Differences in opinion don't automatically lead to this sort of action.

STUDENT: She just said in gym class that she thought the notes were right about me.

COUNSELOR: I'll bring her in and talk to her. We're going to figure this out, I promise.

STUDENT: I just want it to be over with. Thanks, Ms. Meghan.

COUNSELOR: Did you reread "Lost in the Funhouse"? We have some time to talk about that.

STUDENT: I, um, haven't had the chance to read it yet. I will soon.

COUNSELOR: All right, Hannah. We'll talk soon, then.

**Next action:** Follow up with Kimmy Dobson about issues with Hannah. Meet with Hannah again. For lack of a more clinical term, try to crack that shell open.

# Romeo and Juliet

I want to remind Courtney of why we are friends. It's not just because my last name is Geller and hers is Gilmore, or because we both like carrot sticks more than cupcakes. These things are just coincidences, just tiny flowers in our friendship garden, things easily trampled and forgotten.

We're friends because of *Romeo and Juliet*. We're friends because I didn't laugh when the worst thing that ever happened to Courtney, happened.

It was last year, when we were still fourth graders but just barely. It was springtime and the weather was warm, and the way the sun hit the playground had the whole class thinking about next year, when we'd be in fifth grade. We felt more grown-up. This was the same time that Mrs. Gayle the music teacher put up the cast list for the school play. All the fourth and fifth graders had to be in it, which meant a whole bunch of us (including me) had been cast as townspeople and trees. But not Courtney. In swirly purple font, she was Juliet.

She read her name and jumped about four feet into the air with her arms and legs curled out to the side.

"I'm Juliet," she sang.

"I'm tree number six," I said.

"Did you see who my Romeo is?"

I read the list again. "John Block."

"The cutest fifth-grade boy. And he gets to fall in love with me." Courtney twirled so hard, her skirt blew out like a pinwheel.

"It's pretend," I reminded her.

"For now."

She kissed her hand and pressed it to the cast list where it said ROMEO–JOHN BLOCK. The crunch of the paper under her palm hit my ears like a sad-day sound, and I didn't know why.

At the first rehearsal Mrs. Gayle had us read through the play.

"Everyone has at least one line," she said. "So pay attention while we read."

The thing about Shakespeare talk is that it's hard. All the words make sense on their own but turn to mush when you put them together. It's a pretty mush, though, the kind that makes you want to listen even if you don't understand it. "Lost in the Funhouse" is a little like that.

I sat on one side of the stage with the rest of the trees, and Courtney was on the other side with the leads. John Block was next to her, wearing a T-shirt with a bear on it. I tried to see him like Courtney did but couldn't find anything remarkable. Nothing worth "Romeo-oh-Romeo"-ing over.

We were halfway through the play when we got to a scene where Romeo climbs up a balcony to meet Juliet while calling her the sun and talking about broken windows. I read along with the lines and saw the little stage direction underneath: ROMEO KISSES JULIET.

"On the cheek," Mrs. Gayle said. Courtney's face turned as pink as cotton candy, and John's had no color at all. The girls giggled, and the boys punched each other.

Me, I was suddenly over-aware of my dry lips, and how my very first zit was growing right at the corner of my mouth.

"Hannah?"

I looked up at Mrs. Gayle, who was pointing to the script.

"Your line," she said.

Right after a fifth-grade boy kissed my best friend on the cheek, tree number six was supposed to say: "It was meant to be."

I delivered my line in my best tree-number-six voice, and then spent the rest of the read-through imagining the bear on John's shirt coming to life and swallowing Courtney whole.

"I don't get why Mrs. Gayle won't let us rehearse the kiss," Courtney said at lunch a few weeks later. Ryan dropped his head to the cafeteria table, and I laughed. He could barely stand to sit with us anymore. All Courtney talked about was *Romeo and Juliet*. Well, mostly Romeo.

"She told you, Court. Nine-year-olds don't need to practice kissing over and over. Even on the cheek," I remind her.

"I'm not nine up there, though. I'm Juliet, and I would die for my one true love."

If this were a story, I'd go back in time and steal Shakespeare's manuscript for *Romeo and Juliet*. In a dark chamber with only a lantern to guide me and a feather to write with, I would change Juliet's ending. She'd decide not to die for love and instead become an architect or an actress or an author with the power to make her own stories.

"Please, stop," Ryan whined. He threw his hands into the air like they were branches, and froze.

"Looking good, tree number two," I said. I lifted my own arms, bending them a little at the elbows. We did a few more tree poses and laughed together and went back to being Geller, Gilmore, and Grant for the rest of lunch.

That afternoon at rehearsal we all had to try on our costumes. Mine was a brown turtleneck and a green hat with fake leaves hot-glued to the top. Courtney had a cranberry- colored dress and matching veil. We studied ourselves in the mirror.

"Won't John love me in this?" Courtney asked, and curtsied to herself.

"He doesn't have a choice. The script tells him to," I said.

Courtney's eyebrows pulled together in the mirror. "It's like you're not even happy for me. Are you jealous that I'm Juliet?"

I couldn't tell her that I was the opposite of jealous, and that it felt like something was wrong with me. Ever since I'd read ROMEO KISSES JULIET, all I'd been was scared. Scared of growing up and kissing some Romeo and loving him so much that I couldn't live without him.

"No. I'm not jealous."

"Good."

Courtney took me by the arm (technically my branch) into the hallway. John Block was sipping from the water fountain in a white shirt with puffy sleeves and a brown vest on top. He picked up his head and saw us standing there.

"You look nice, Courtney," he said, and wiped his mouth with his hand. I swear I'd never noticed just how wet lips can look.

"Thanks, Romeo—I mean, John."

He smiled a little bit and waved good-bye. We stayed quiet in the hall until we couldn't see him anymore. Courtney turned to me and squealed. I squealed too, but it sounded more like an animal in pain.

• • •

On the night of the show, I peeked around the edge of the curtain into the gym, where all the parents sat in metal folding chairs. Mom and Dad were a few rows back with Ryan's parents, reading a program. Courtney's parents sat in the front row. Mrs. Gilmore had her camera pointed and ready to go. I let the curtain swing back into place and took my spot with the other trees.

Courtney walked onto the stage, past the white masking tape $X$ that told her where to start, and over to me. She pulled me by the arm (branch) into the corner.

"Smell my face," she demanded.

"What?"

"Smell me!"

I leaned closer to the circle of red blush that Mrs. Gayle had painted onto her cheek, and inhaled. Courtney smelled like berries and sugar.

"Very sweet," I said.

"That's what John will smell when he kisses me." She smiled, but her eyes didn't. Other than the polka dots of blush, Courtney was as pale as a cloud.

"Are you okay?" I asked.

Little lines formed around Courtney's eyes, and her jaw clenched tight like there were tears inside her that needed to burst free. She nodded.

"It's okay to be nervous. You'll be great," I reassured her. She stomped her foot.

"I'm not nervous." She turned away from me and went to stand on the white $X$. I felt shivery, even when the curtains opened, and I hoped that I'd just look like a tree rustling in the wind.

The play was going fine. Everyone stumbled over the Shakespeare language, but in a good way that let the audience know we were trying. Ryan delivered his line, "It's a cold night tonight," at the end of the big party in the play, and Mrs. Grant stood up to clap and cheer. She cheered so loudly that eventually the rest of the audience joined in. Ryan bowed, and we had to wait until the clapping stopped to keep going with the play.

The time came for Romeo to cross the stage to the balcony made of a cardboard box, where Juliet waited.

"What light through yonder window breaks? It

is the east, and Juliet is the sun," John recited. He leaned over the ledge toward Courtney. She closed her eyes, and his lips touched her cheek. She was supposed to pull away shyly, put her hand to her face, and smile. Instead her arms dropped to her stomach.

And instead of looking into John's eyes and delivering her next line, she opened her mouth, leaned over the ledge, and threw up all over his shoes.

Some of the trees and townspeople gasped. Some laughed. John jumped back like Courtney was a monster. I didn't know what to do, so I said my line.

"It was meant to be."

The curtains flew shut. From the other side Mrs. Gayle announced that we would take an intermission. Courtney ran off with her hand over her mouth. John left too. His shoes made a trail of her puke on the stage.

If this were a story, I wouldn't want to read it.

"Everyone, into the cafeteria. We'll be back on when we get this cleaned up," Mrs. Gayle said. On the way to the cafeteria, Ryan and I looked at each other out of the corners of our eyes but didn't say anything. The rest of the trees laughed about "Pukey

Gilmore" and said lines from the play with gagging noises added in. I didn't see Courtney anywhere.

"Cover for me," I said to Ryan, and took off before Mrs. Gayle or her helpers saw me. I checked the bathroom first.

"Courtney?"

"You mean Pukey?" Kimmy was at a sink, laughing.

"No, I meant Courtney." I looked under the stall doors for feet.

"I don't know a Courtney, but Pukey ran outside."

I glared at Kimmy.

"Maybe if you were nicer, people would actually like you," I said to her, and headed for the door before I could regret being a mean girl like other people in our class.

The doors led out to the playground, where the sky was all kinds of pink and purple, and shadows covered the swings. Everything looked so different in the dark.

"Courtney?" I called out. I listened past the bird-calls and the crickets and the springtime sounds.

"I'm here," she answered. Her voice came from behind the dumpsters. I crossed the four-square courts and hopscotch lines to join her. She was sitting with her back against the dumpster. The veil was coming loose from her hair. She didn't smell like berries anymore.

"I can't go back in there," she whispered into the ground. I sat down on the gravel in front of her.

"You have to finish the show," I said.

"Everyone is making fun of me." She dropped her head onto her knees.

"They've all gotten sick too. Did you eat something bad?"

A tear sparkled like a star down Courtney's face.

"I wasn't sick. I was scared." She drew a heart in the dirt with her finger and then wiped it away.

"Scared of what?"

"The kiss. John. But I don't want to be scared, Hannah. I want to be a grown-up."

I held my arms out to Courtney, and she slipped inside. I hugged her while she cried over things that I'd learned about from my Judy Blume books. I couldn't let her give up before she got to her ending.

"Let's go back inside," I said.

"How can I show my face?"

"The same way as always, right?"

• • •

Courtney finished the play, and the rest of the school year, while being called Pukey Gilmore. Eventually Joanie Lawson had her incident during the summer movie night, and there was someone new to tease. People started to forget about what had happened during *Romeo and Juliet*, but Courtney never did. If I can remind her that I was there when other people were calling her names, maybe I can get her back. Maybe she'll hold her arms out to me and I can cry over everything.

Courtney's sitting with Rebecca in the cafeteria. I'm with Ryan in our normal place. He devours his cheeseburger while I can't take one bite.

"What's wrong?" he asks.

"I need to talk to Courtney," I say.

"Yeah, go get the third piece of our puzzle back," he says. I wait until Rebecca gets up to throw her trash away, and then I approach their segment of the green table.

"Can I sit here?" I ask Courtney.

"I guess," she answers to her peanut-butter-banana sandwich. I sit.

"I don't want to fight anymore," I say.

117

"We're not fighting. There's just too much going on with you."

"You're supposed to be my friend. You're supposed to be there until it blows over."

"It's not only this. I don't understand you," she says. I see Rebecca making her way back to the table. I'm running out of time.

"But what about when everyone called you Pukey Gilmore? I didn't leave you," I say.

Courtney looks up from the sandwich, and I can almost taste regret. Her blue eyes go dark like the ocean at night. If this were a story, I would drown in them.

"Get away from me," she says, and I do.

It was a mistake to bring up *Romeo and Juliet*. I should know better than anyone else how much it hurts to remember.

# Dinner for Two

Dad is working late on a project, so Mom and I make spaghetti and meatballs for dinner. When it's just the two of us, we pull up stools and eat at the kitchen counter. We watch cartoons while we eat and leave the dirty dishes everywhere. It's my favorite kind of mess. Mom's bun is loose and relaxed tonight.

"How was school?" Mom asks.

"Good," I say.

"What's going on with the notes?"

I look down into my plate. If this were a story, I'd be able to turn a meatball into a cave in the middle of the Marinara Sea. I would hide there until the storm passed, making friends with the long spaghetti eels.

"They might know who did it," I say.

"Who was it?"

"Kimmy Dobson. Ms. Meghan says she's going to talk to her tomorrow," I say. Mom nods.

"She's a tough kid. Can't be easy to live the way

she does, but it's no excuse. I'm glad they figured it out," Mom says. She reaches across the counter to run her hand through my hair. I try to smile past the meatball-size lump in my throat.

"Me too."

In the background a cartoon cat hits a cartoon dog in the head with a hammer. Stars and stripes and baby bluebirds spin around the dog's head. He falls to the ground. The impact should kill him, but he's still there, still holding on, still fighting.

"That dog reminds me of you, Mom," I say. She looks to the TV and narrows her eyes at the wounded cartoon character.

"That's funny. Why would you say that?"

"You never give up."

Mom tucks a piece of hair behind my ear. "Your dad should be home from his renovation soon. Let's get this kitchen clean," she says.

I'd like to call in a team to renovate my brain. They can smash the walls that hold everything in. They can paint over the bad memories. They can flutter around like fireflies until I'm a brand-new Hannah.

Before we can start clearing the dishes, the front

door opens and Dad walks in. His blue T-shirt and jeans and work boots are stained by gray paint. My heart thumps with panicked beats. The mess in the kitchen might as well be the town dump.

But there's a big, fat grin on Dad's face.

"Hi, Michael. We were just about to—ooh—" Mom starts to greet Dad, before he swoops her up into his arms. He spins her around like they're doing a dance routine, and then lets her go to come hug me.

"It went great, guys. We're going to be set for a long, long time," Dad announces.

"That's wonderful. You worked so hard for that project," Mom says.

"Go, Dad," I contribute. My bones feel like fizzy bubbles in a soda, all full of happiness.

"We'll celebrate at bowling this week. Deluxe nachos for everyone." Dad bowls every Friday with his league. Mom and I don't go with him all the time, but I like when we do, because everyone says what a beautiful family we are, and it makes me believe that we could be, if the sad sounds would just leave us alone.

The idea of deluxe nachos makes me think about

the dirty dishes, so I start to put them in the sink, but the bubbles inside me are too excited, and a plate slips out of my hand. One of Dad's old-fashioned Packers plates. It shatters into pieces on the ground. I can almost hear the happy bubbles pop.

"I'm so sorry," I blurt.

"That's okay, Hannah. We have four more of those," Dad says. He gets the broom from the closet, and I get the dustpan from under the sink. I hold the dustpan steady, and he sweeps the broken pieces in, the grin still wide on his face. It makes me smile too.

I'm ready to be a beautiful family. I'm ready for things to get better.


"I think I know why I hear sounds so clearly. And why I can talk to you and other things," I say to Ambrose that night. I lie on my stomach in bed with "Lost in the Fun-house" in front of me. Ambrose is perched on my back.

"Why?" he asks.

"Right here it says Ambrose had receivers in his mind and it allowed things to talk to him. They made him understand things he shouldn't. That's it. I have receivers too."

"You must," he says.

"I think mine are acting up, though. I'm going to fix them so that all I hear are the happy sounds."

"So, start tomorrow. Retune them," Ambrose replies. I sit up in excitement, and Ambrose flies off my back. He lands on the floor.

"Now I need to be fixed," he mumbles. I giggle and pick him back up. I hold him close to my heart.

"Ambrose, if I fix my receivers, does that mean I won't be able to hear you anymore?"

"I'll always be here for you," he says.

I try to ignore the fact that he didn't really say no.

# Importunate. Spiteful. Acute.

In class we practice spelling. Mrs. Bloom goes over the words on the board.

IMPORTUNATE.

SPITEFUL.

ACUTE.

The thing about spelling is, you don't need to know the definition of a word to spell it. But I like meanings. I think looking at a word only for how its spelled is like judging a person by their outsides.

We're copying the words into our vocabulary journals when there's a knock on the door. Ms. Meghan is standing at the back of the classroom.

"Keep copying," Mrs. Bloom says, and joins her.

"Importunate" describes something that is persistent.

"Spiteful" means something unkind.

"Acute" is when something is felt very intensely.

Mrs. Bloom and Ms. Meghan talk in the back of the class. I snap the tip of my pencil on purpose and walk to the sharpener near where they are standing. I hope my newly repaired receivers can hear them.

Before I make it to the sharpener, Mrs. Bloom is tapping Kimmy on the shoulder. She motions for Kimmy to follow her. Kimmy's eyes are wide when she puts down her pencil. They look wet by the time she's taken out the door.

If this were a story, a big red arrow would appear above my head, so that everyone would know I am to blame.

I put my pencil into the sharpener.

"It's over now," I say under my breath.

"Yooouuuu diiiiiid theeeeee riiiiiiiight thiiiiiing," the sharpener whirrs at me. I pull the pencil out, and the voice stops. No one's looking at me. No one else has heard.

I put the pencil back in. "You—" Pencil out.

Quiet.

Pencil in. "Did—" Pencil out.

Quiet.

Pencil in—

"Hannah? Stop playing with the sharpener," Mrs. Bloom says.

Pencil out.

I go back to my seat and start copying the words again.

Sometimes when you learn vocabulary, it's useful to put the words into a sentence.

Maybe I did do the right thing, but the *importunate* reminders the *spiteful* notes have left me with an *acute* pain in the center of my chest.

# Counselor's Notes:
# Thursday, October 29

**Name:** Kimmy Dobson

**Grade:** Five

**Reason for visit:** Discussion of classroom incident involving notes against Hannah. Kimmy has been suspected of being responsible for said notes. There is a history of competition between the two.

**Demeanor:** Kimmy shows little consideration for personal appearance. Features are clouded by expression of anger. Pushes chair back from table to increase distance. Behavior is consistent with what has been demonstrated since recent death of her mother, and subsequent move to live with her grandmother.

**Visit:** Transcript follows.

> COUNSELOR: Do you know why you're here?
>
> STUDENT: I have no idea.
>
> COUNSELOR: You know there's been some bullying going on in your class.
>
> STUDENT: Yeah. You came and talked to us.

COUNSELOR: Do you have any feelings about the notes?

STUDENT: Why would I?

COUNSELOR: I know you and Hannah haven't always gotten along.

STUDENT: Did she tell you that I wrote them? Did she?

COUNSELOR: You're not being accused of anything.

STUDENT: Hannah is thoughtless and weird. But I didn't write any notes about her, I swear.

COUNSELOR: Let's forget about that for a minute. How have you been doing? How long has it been since your mom died, now?

STUDENT: A year.

COUNSELOR: How have you been feeling?

STUDENT: It feels like she's been gone forever. Like I never had her at all.

COUNSELOR: It would be understandable if you wrote these notes out of pain.

STUDENT: I didn't write them!

COUNSELOR: Okay, Kimmy, okay. I want you to calm down before I send you back to class. What can I do to help?

*Student points to dictionary on shelf.*

STUDENT: Can you quiz me?

**Next action:** Despite Kimmy's clear anger and feelings of helplessness, it is still unclear whether she wrote the notes. However, she may need more consistent sessions to combat her volatile feelings.

# A Pink Trailer

**K**immy doesn't come to school on Friday. When the day is over, I take a detour before going home. The crossing guard watches me walk halfway down my street, and then I cut through the neighbor's yard into the woods. The October air is starting to fade to make room for November. November air feels like spices, strong and bitter and sweet. Skin remembers what true cold feels like.

White branches crisscross above my head, and fallen leaves slide under my feet. I use the stepping stones that break the surface of the stream to cross to the other side. The woods are quiet except for the wind and rushing water.

Sometimes when you're in the woods, you take a breath and you're somewhere else, experiencing some other day when the air smelled exactly the same. You realize that you're a collection of memories all strung together. The you that you were a few weeks ago and one year ago and ten years ago are all the same, no matter how much time goes by, no matter how many things are different. I like to think that when I'm a hundred, I might be able to breathe in deeply and remember who I am right now.

It doesn't take long to get to the trailer park. The homes are spread out in the grass, across the street from where the school buses are parked at the end of the day. One dirt road cuts through the middle.

Kimmy's trailer is pale pink with white shutters. There's a plastic ghost stuck to the door and a pumpkin on the front steps. It's already rotting, just a day before Halloween. Looking at it makes me feel empty.

The door to the trailer opens, and Kimmy steps out. She has orange-and-black garlands in her arms. I watch her wrap the strands around the rusted rails on her front steps. The October wind blows her green checkered shirt. She doesn't have a jacket.

I know I should leave my hiding spot in the trees, but I can't look away. She puts a black cat decoration right under the ghost. She rests a small scarecrow against the rotting pumpkin. There's not enough room on the door or the rails or the little front stoop, so the decorations all lean against each other.

If this were a story, a bus from a home-makeover reality show would roll into the trailer park. The host would call out to Kimmy and her grandma. In just five minutes the crew would demolish the trailer into a million pieces and build a mansion from the ruins. Kimmy would have a whole room just to practice spelling in, and there would be plenty of space on their new front porch for Halloween decorations. Sometimes it hurts to remember that this is not a story.

Even if Kimmy is a bully, maybe I'm not much better. I threw pennies at her in the grocery store. I told Ms. Meghan that she wrote the notes, when I didn't know for sure if she did.

When she's done decorating, she walks down her steps and observes her work. I don't know what Kimmy sees when she looks at it, but she drops to the dirt ground. She sits cross-legged in front of the pink trailer and puts her face in her hands. I wait for a few minutes, but no one calls her inside. No one says it's too cold to be outside in just a green checkered shirt.

I want to go over and tell her that the garlands glitter even though the sky is gray, but I know she wouldn't want to hear from me. I have done enough.

# From Hannah's Pages of "Lost in the Funhouse"

Suppose the lights came on now!

# The Girl in the Arcade

We go to Dad's bowling league with him that night. His teammates mess up my hair and tell me how old I've gotten. I know it's rude to say the same thing to them, so I just smile.

The bowling alley smells like feet and french fries. I take out my vocabulary list to study.

"Mom, will you quiz me?" I ask. She has lipstick on, which she only does when we go to the bowling alley. She's not wearing a bun tonight; instead her hair rests on her shoulders in shiny, black curls.

"Of course," she says. She takes my list and looks it over. "'Aptitude.'"

"A-p-t-i-t-u-d-e."

"That's right. Good job."

Dad has an aptitude for bowling. If this were a story, Dad would be an Olympic bowler, but he's just the champion of his league. It makes him happy the same way stories and words make me happy.

Mom quizzes me while Dad plays. Each time he

knocks all the pins down, he comes over and kisses Mom. He gets a little bit of lipstick on his mouth, but he doesn't seem to mind.

"'Tenacious,'" Mom says.

"*T-e-n-a-c-i-o-u-s*," I say.

"Got it."

"That means 'strong-willed.'"

"I know that one. That's you," Mom says.

"You think I'm strong?" I ask.

"Of course you are, hon."

I've never thought that I might be strong, because of the way I get sad and let my mind wander. But maybe it does take strength to have all that inside me and still not give up. Maybe Ambrose was strong too. It must have been scary to be lost in the funhouse. He could have waited in a dark corner until someone came to find him, but he kept moving, even if that meant he got farther away from where he was supposed to be.

The bowling teams start a new game, and I leave the table for the arcade. The room is lit in neon and strobe lights, so everything looks dim. The prizes in the crane game have been the same for years. The arcade is empty, but the machines chime anyway, calling out to me with bells and pings and voices. It's one of those places that goes untouched, that exists without anyone really noticing it's there.

I see what I'm looking for on the floor by the shooting game. A penny flashes in the colored lights, and I inspect it. Heads up. I take the coin and tuck it into my pocket. My career as a coin dropper started in the arcade, when I had my first urge to get the pennies out of the dark and replant them somewhere brighter. I find two more by the pinball machine and think about how hard it is to forget the past when it's always right there just waiting for you to grab it.

There are two sections to the arcade, so I leave the front part with the games and walk into the back with the air hockey tables and black lights. My white Converse sneakers glow blue, and I use them to guide me to another penny across the floor. I turn and look up to see something else illuminated in the dark corner of the room. A T-shirt. A flash of white teeth. A girl with her back pushed up against the wall, and a boy with his lips on her cheek.

"Stop, stop, there's someone here," the girl says,

but he doesn't stop. Her eyes squeeze shut like she's having a nightmare. The boy's hands move up the wall on either side of her, and the girl disappears behind him. I run from the back room. The coins in my hand fall and bounce against the floor. A sad-day sound like shattering glass.

"Don't go, Hannah," the pinball machine calls out when I pass.

"Nothing's changed. We're still the same," the crane game says.

When Ambrose saw confusing things, they became new pieces of the jumbled-up puzzle inside him. I won't forget the girl's face flushed white in the black light. I wish I knew her story.

I rush back to the table and notice that the bowling teams have gotten quieter. Dad's score is a line of red *X*s, which means he's gotten all strikes. When a bowler is on the way to a perfect game, it's tradition not to speak to him. Even one word could disrupt the rhythm and ruin everything.

Dad keeps rolling strikes. I try not to pay attention because it makes me nervous. I hope for the girl to come out of the arcade, but she doesn't. Across the bowling alley, a woman with dark hair shaped like a mushroom walks toward the exit that is next to our table, and my breath gets sucked from my lungs. It's Ms. Meghan, and she sees me too.

"Hi there, Hannah," she says. She has a red balloon in her hand.

"What's that?" I ask, and point to it.

Ms. Meghan laughs. "I was here for my nephew's birthday party. Every guest gets a balloon." She tugs at the string. I look at Mom. She crosses her arms like she's making a shield.

"We're here watching my husband," Mom says, and points to Dad. He's bent over retying his bowling shoes. He looks in our direction when he sits back up.

"Hello, Mr. Geller," Ms. Meghan says.

I swear I hear Dad's whole bowling league gasp. Mom clears her throat and smiles at him. I grip the sticky table. If this were a story, Dad and the other bowlers would turn into cavemen with war-painted faces. They would attack Ms. Meghan with spears as if she were a mammoth and then feed her to their god: the machine that collects the pins after someone knocks them down.

"Hello," Dad says, and turns back to his team.

Ms. Meghan tugs on the balloon string again. Her eyes look like there's still a kid hiding inside them.

"Have I said something?" she asks.

"Dad is about to bowl a three hundred. You're not supposed to talk to him," I say.

"I'm so sorry."

"You didn't know," Mom says.

"It's a *s-u-p-e-r-s-t-i-t-i-o-n*," I tell her. Ms. Meghan nods, and she reminds me of a fish out of water, thrown from her peach office. Her tank.

When will the girl come out of the arcade?

"I should thank you for your help with the notes situation. I'm glad it's been resolved," Mom says.

"We're still looking into it," Ms. Meghan says.

"It hasn't been settled?"

"I'd rather not discuss that here. Please do tell your husband that I'm sorry for disturbing his mojo. Good night."

"I'll be calling to follow up," Mom says. Ms. Meghan nods and puts her hood over her pom-pom hair. She slips out the automatic doors, bringing in a gust of cold air. But my arms are already covered in goose bumps.

*We're still looking into it.*

Dad steps up to the lane for his last roll. His bowling ball is the color of seaweed. He swings his arm back, then forward as he releases the ball. It streaks down the center of the lane and then curves just slightly. Mom grabs my hand and squeezes too hard.

The lead pin falls into the pyramid of pins behind it, taking them out as it flies backward. There is one pin left wobbling in the corner, until the lead pin comes rolling back across the lane to knock it over.

The bowling alley bursts into applause. Dad's name is announced over the loudspeaker. Mom smiles so hard, I think she might sprain her cheeks. I smile back, but I'm still thinking about Ms. Meghan.

*We're still looking into it.*

When we walk outside, Dad holds up the trophy he received for scoring a three hundred. It shines in the orange glow from the streetlights.

"I can't believe it," Dad says.

"I can," Mom murmurs.

"What did the counselor want?"

"Just saying hi."

"Hey, Hannah. How do you spell 'champion'?" Dad asks me. I roll my eyes. He knows that word is too easy.

"*D-a-d-d-y*," I chant.

"That's my girl."

He opens the doors of the truck for Mom and me. The leather seats are cold even through my jeans. I try my hardest to be happy. Dad is okay and no one is yelling and Mom thinks I'm strong, but the girl never came out of the arcade.

*We're still looking into it.*

# Trick or Treat

Ryan arrives at our door on Halloween wearing a pin-striped baseball uniform and carrying a glove. He takes in my boxy costume, painted white with the letter *H*.

"What are you?" he asks.

"I'm a Scrabble piece," I say.

"Do people still play Scrabble?"

Ambrose and I played a game last night. The costume was his idea. But I can't tell Ryan that my talking stuffed elephant was the inspiration.

"Where'd you get your costume?" I ask.

"It was my dad's in the eighties. The glove, too," he says.

My heart swells with thankfulness for Ryan, who smiles even if his costume is a hand-me-down.

"Do you want to start the candy consumption process?" I ask him.

"Only you would say 'consumption' instead of 'eating.' But of course."

When Ryan brings up my big words, it's not to be mean. It's to show he knows me well. We go to the candy bowl on the kitchen table and reach in.

"Those are for the trick-or-treaters," Mom says from the couch.

"We are trick-or-treaters," I reply. She smiles in a way that still means business.

"One piece." She turns back to the Halloween movie she's watching. The broken TV hasn't been replaced yet, so the witches fly across a crack in the sky.

I hear footsteps on the stairs. Dad walks in wearing a leather vest and a red bandana.

"Biker Dad is ready to go," he announces. He poses with his arms crossed.

"You look tough, Mr. Geller," Ryan says, and Dad gives him a high five.

Dad looks over at Mom on the couch.

"Why don't you come with us?" he asks.

"Someone has to stay for the trick-or-treaters."

"Is there a kid more important than Hannah?"

The receivers in my head start picking up static, like they sense sad-day sounds lurking somewhere in the airwaves.

"That's not what I mean, Michael," Mom says. Dad turns to me. His biker outfit suddenly looks more intimidating than goofy.

"Hannah, don't you want your mother to come?"

I look at the candy bowl and feel everyone else looking at me. I'm stuck in the middle of the conflict like the caramel center of a chocolate bar.

"It's okay. We just want to get to the candy before it's gone," I say. I take the plastic pumpkins from the counter and hand one to Ryan. Then I grab his arm and drag him to the door with me.

"Bye, Ms. Boring," I hear Dad say to Mom before he follows behind us. It sounds mean, like it should be written on one of the bullying notes. I don't want to hear anything else. My fixed receivers are still too fragile.

"Race you," Ryan says, and takes off. His solution for all problems is to race them away. *That means he thinks my parents are a problem.* I chase the thought off and sprint after Ryan into the dark.

Dad catches up with us in the street. I take one last look at our house from the bottom of the driveway and see Mom at the door. The light from inside turns her into a trapped shadow.

"Where's your girl Courtney?" Dad asks as we walk.

"She had other plans," I say.

Ryan nudges me in the arm.

"They don't know you're fighting?" he asks quietly. I shake my head.

We walk to the busy neighborhood a few blocks away from mine, where the houses are big and the grown-ups give out full-size candy bars. My bones can tell that it's Halloween. A spooky cold permeates the air.

"When do you think we'll be too old for trick-or-treating?" Ryan asks me.

"Why should stocking up on candy have an expiration date?" I answer. He laughs.

"Maybe next year when we get to middle school," he says.

I think about my pen pal, Ashley, and the Halloween party she told me about, where she'll be dressed as Madonna. For the first time since we started writing to each other, I worry that she might not like me. The Scrabble piece costume starts to feel heavy.

"Yeah, maybe then," I reply.

If this were a story, the moonlit, masked creatures in the street would be real. The pirates and fairies and zombies would coexist despite their differences. Maybe that's not so much like a story. People do that every day.

"Mike," someone calls out from the dark. A round man shuffles down the street toward us. There's a tiny girl dressed as an angel running behind him.

"Is that you, Dave?" Dad shouts back.

"You got me." Dave shakes Dad's hand. I recognize Dave from the bowling alley. The little angel hides behind his legs.

"Enjoying the night?" Dad asks.

"Couldn't be better. You want a smoke?"

Dad looks at me and Ryan.

"Can you two go on your own?" he asks.

"Sure, Dad," I answer.

"Take Ruby with you," Dave says, and pushes the angel out from behind him. Her eyes get round, and I notice in the streetlights that they're similar in color to shiny pennies.

"Yeah, Ruby, come with us," I say. She hesitates

but follows Ryan and me. I watch Dave hand Dad a cigar and light the end. It burns cherry red.

I try to talk to Ruby.

"What grade are you in?" I ask her.

"Mrs. Thyme," she says instead. My third-grade teacher.

"Ryan and I had her too."

Ruby slips her hand into mine unexpectedly.

"My dad's not supposed to smoke," she whispers.

"Mine either," I answer.

I want to tell Ruby more ways that she and I are similar. I recognize her quietness and the way she looks at everything with full-moon eyes.

If this were a ghost story, Ruby would do something to show me that she is really a reincarnation of me as a third grader, like she'd quote "Lost in the Funhouse" or draw her own word search with chalk on the pavement. She would talk about something that only I could know about, like the worst fight Mom and Dad ever had.

I'm glad this isn't a ghost story, because honestly, that would be terrifying.

"We have to hit that house on the hill. Last year they gave out dollar bills," Ryan says.

"I'd rather have chocolate," Ruby says.

It looks like the whole neighborhood has heard about the dollar bills and is gathered on top of the hill to collect. A line runs down the brick walkway in front of the door. We wait behind two princesses. Ruby notices that Ryan and I don't have candy yet and puts a few peanut butter cups and licorice sticks in each of our buckets.

We're almost to the door when someone cuts in front of us from the shadows. Someone in a green checkered shirt and a Frankenstein mask.

"Dude, you just cut us," Ryan says. The cutter turns around and pulls off the mask.

"I'm not a dude," Kimmy snaps. She notices me, and the look on her face is scarier than any costume.

"Hi, Kimmy," I offer. She reaches out her hand and slaps my plastic pumpkin to the ground. Candy spills over the bricks and onto the wet lawn.

"You told the counselor that I wrote those stupid notes," she snaps at me.

"I . . ."

"I don't care what you say, Hannah. I didn't write them." She takes a step toward me. Ryan gets between us and holds up his baseball glove.

148

"Back off," he warns.

"Make me."

It's Ruby who makes her. She kicks Kimmy in the shin with her white shoe. Not hard enough to send her to the ground, but enough to make her twenty times angrier.

"You're going to be sorry you ever messed with me," Kimmy says.

"Come on. A dollar bill isn't worth this. Let's race," Ryan says. We get out of line and run all the way back down the hill. We catch our breath at the bottom. Little clouds form in front of our mouths.

"What was she talking about?" Ruby asks me.

"Nothing," I say. I don't want her to know about the notes. That information doesn't belong under her halo.

We find Dad in the same spot with Dave. The cigars are gone, but I can still smell them. Smoke hovers like a lost spirit in the air.

"Did you have a good time, angel?" Dave asks Ruby. She's still holding my hand.

"Yes. I kicked a girl in the leg," she says. Dad and Dave look at us, but I just shrug.

"It *is* the night of mischief," I say.

"I'm glad you toughened this little one up," Dave replies.

"Ruby's tenacious. That means 'strong-willed,'" I say. Dave looks confused.

"Hannah likes words," Dad explains.

"Come on, tiger." Dave takes Ruby from me. I wish she didn't have to leave. I try using my magic to bring her plastic pumpkin to life. Something tells me that Ruby would be able to hear it speak, that she's a believer.

We head toward the next neighborhood. Ryan takes his hat off and blocks his face when he whispers to me, "Did you really tell on Kimmy?"

"I thought she wrote them," I say.

"If she didn't, then who did?"

If this were a story, then this part would be the reversal. That's when you think one thing is true, and then something happens and the plot takes a turn.

It's like I'm being catapulted in a new direction.

# As Told by the Plastic Pumpkin

Y ou should talk to Ruby," Hannah whispers
as I walk away. Well, actually, I don't walk.
Ruby does, and I'm along for the ride.

"Okay. I'll tell her those candy bars from the blue
house are expired. Now she won't crack her teeth!" I
answer.

I like to call myself a comedian. The cackle-
lantern. That's a good one, right?

Ruby holds me in front of her face like she can
hear me laughing.

"Pumpkin?"

# Riley Jones

Something happened in second grade that's become a sharp piece of my collection of memories. A boy in our class named Riley Jones died. He ran into the street after a Frisbee, and the minivan driving by didn't have time to stop. I don't know how you're supposed to react to that sort of thing when you're seven, but when we found out, all I could think about was the one time I talked to Riley Jones. He asked me if I wanted to have a handstand competition at recess, and I said yes. When he beat me, I told him I didn't want to have competitions anymore.

Mom and Dad asked me how I felt about the accident a few days after it happened.

"We had a handstand competition during recess," I said.

"Do you want to talk about it?"

"No. I'll be fine."

I replayed my one memory of Riley over and over until I was clogged up with sadness. I constructed the feeling of losing a friend, like an unstable gingerbread house. It was the first time that I realized how real things could become in a person's head. I wondered if maybe the universe itself was created by people's overthinking.

A month later a tree was planted for Riley in front of the school. It was thin with small white flowers on the branches. There was a ceremony where we all dropped our heads and took a moment of silence for Riley. I used the time to think about our handstand competition, to miss the boy who had lived for only seven years, to imagine him dying in the street. A bird landed on one of the branches and sang, a happy sound for a sad day.

It scared me how sad I could be, how I could own heartbreak like a T-shirt or a choker necklace and keep it all buried inside me. I thought maybe Riley could live forever if his being gone hurt enough.

The tree is still there. It blooms with white flowers every spring. When I see it, I think about Riley and me turning the world upside down together.

If this were a story, this part would be the emotional development. It's supposed to help you understand why a character is the way she is. I hope so at least.

# As Told by the Stop Sign

I can't go in there," Hannah whispers. To the world. She looks. Worried this morning when she. Crosses the street. She is. Bent over like she. Has a lot of weight on her back. My weather calculations tell me that it. Has nothing to do with the pressure of the wind.

I've watched Hannah. Cross that same street. From this same crossing guard's hand. Since she was barely as tall as me. Her shoulders have never hung quite so. Low. I know a lot about traffic laws and history and octagonal shapes, but. I don't know why Hannah needs help this morning.

It goes against everything. I'm designed for to tell her:

"Just go."

Hannah looks around. I don't think she expects that. It is me. After all, I'm a big. Red. Stop sign.

"Just go," I try again, and her eyes fall. On me. I straighten myself. As much as I can.

"I can't," she says when she. Walks past and no one. Is looking.

I've learned from my years in this job. That stopping doesn't get you. Anywhere.

"Yes, you can. Go."

She is behind me now. I can't see what she decides to do. Stop or go. There are other kids. To help cross the street. Other footsteps fading away but. I pretend they are Hannah's. I hope that she decides. To persevere.

# Counselor's Notes: Thursday, April 30

**Name:** Hannah Geller

**Grade:** Three

**Reason for visit:** Emotional outburst and worrisome comments that are outside Hannah's normal realm of behavior.

**Demeanor:** Hannah seemed surprised to be in the office, and confused by her own actions. Got off topic easily, as if she finds one thread in a sentence to pull apart and analyze. More observant than average student at this grade level. Shows evidence of literary gifts.

**Visit:** Transcript follows.

> COUNSELOR: Can you tell me why you were crying, Hannah?
>
> STUDENT: I already told Mrs. Thyme.
>
> COUNSELOR: I'd like to hear too, if you don't mind.
>
> STUDENT: Why?
>
> COUNSELOR: I'm here to help.

STUDENT: Do you forget things?

COUNSELOR: Sure. Sometimes on accident, and sometimes I forget things on purpose.

STUDENT: Did you know that a brain can only hold a certain amount of information? Kind of like a computer.

COUNSELOR: I did know that.

STUDENT: Well, I don't think that's true with me. I remember everything.

COUNSELOR: Like what?

STUDENT: Like how I couldn't sleep at my first sleepover because there was a shadow on the wall that looked like a ghost, and what I ate for breakfast the day that Riley Jones died.

COUNSELOR: That must be taking up a lot of room.

STUDENT: I have unlimited storage.

COUNSELOR: Why were you crying, Hannah? What were you remembering?

STUDENT: The . . . astronauts.

COUNSELOR: Try to stay on topic.

STUDENT: I am. The astronauts were on TV.

Mom wouldn't turn the TV down, and Dad didn't like it.

COUNSELOR: What happened?

STUDENT: They fought. They fight a lot.

COUNSELOR: I understand. You don't have to say anything else.

STUDENT: Thank you.

COUNSELOR: Do you like to read, Hannah?

STUDENT: I love to read.

COUNSELOR: I do too. When I was in college, I read a story called "Lost in the Funhouse." The main character really stuck with me. It's way above third-grade-level reading, so I can't give you all of it, but I'm going to give you some parts of the story to look at. I think you might like it.

STUDENT: I'm sure I will.

**Next action:** Call parents.

# As Told by Ambrose

*D*o you remember the day we met, Ambrose?"
Hannah asks me.

"Of course I do."

I met Hannah two years ago, after Ms. Meghan
called and asked Hannah's parents about the fighting.
Her dad held me around the ribs and brought me up
the stairs into her bedroom. He sat on the edge of her
bed and ran a hand over her hair.

"Hannah?"

Hannah rolled over and opened her eyes. She sat
up when she saw her dad there.

"What's wrong?" she asked.

"Nothing's wrong. I brought you something." He
handed me to Hannah. She scooped me up and held
me out in front of her.

The thing about being a stuffed animal is, you
never know whether the kid will want you or not. I
could tell right away that Hannah didn't want me.
She needed me.

"I'll call him Ambrose."

"What's that from?"

"A story." She tucked me under the comforter with her, and I was home. Her dad took a breath and adjusted Hannah's pillow.

"There's something we have to talk about. The counselor told us you were upset that your mother and I fight. But I promise you, Hannah, we're going to be fine."

"Okay, Daddy."

"You won't talk to anyone about this anymore, then, right?"

She crushed me tighter into her chest.

"Right."

For as long as I've known Hannah, she has kept that promise.

# Unable to Forget

I'm in Ms. Meghan's office again. She has given me a piece of paper and a set of crayons to draw with. She watches me from across the table.

If this were a story, Ms. Meghan would hold up cards with different shapes of ink blots. I would say that one looked like an arcade game, and another looked like a willow tree, and another like a rotting pumpkin. She would write in her notes that I was crazy and send me away to the abandoned insane asylum on the other side of town, where kids go to scare themselves at night.

"I'm sorry it's been so long since we've really talked, Hannah," Ms. Meghan says.

"That's okay." I don't want to be here. Being in Ms. Meghan's office feels like standing on the edge of a mountain called Truth Point and being told to jump off without a parachute.

"I was hoping we'd have the bullying resolved, but it's gotten more complicated now."

I nod, and start to draw the objects that have spoken to me. Ambrose. Penny. The pencil sharpener. The plastic pumpkin. The crossing guard's stop sign, which this morning called out to me to "go."

"Hannah, can you write your name on that piece of paper for me?" she asks.

I write my name in the middle of the paper.

"Kimmy says she didn't write the notes," Ms. Meghan continues, and takes a sip of coffee.

"How do you know she's telling the truth?" I ask.

"I don't know for sure."

I color the final shades of blue into a swatch of sky.

"Hannah, I want to talk for a few minutes about your parents," Ms. Meghan says. I press the blue crayon into the paper a little too hard, and the tip crumbles into waxy shavings.

"Dad still scored a perfect game that night you talked to him," I say.

She half-smiles at me. "I'm glad."

The drawings start to get blurry.

"That's not what you want to hear, is it?" I ask.

"Do you remember why you came to see me that first time?"

"Because I cried in the line to music class."

"But why? Why were you crying?"

I remember that day. My class was walking in a straight line to the music room. The floor was squeaky clean and everything was normal, but then my chest broke open. I felt leaky and bruised. Mrs. Thyme saw me and took me out of line and asked what was wrong. I told her that lately there were more sad days than happy days, but she didn't understand what I meant. I didn't blame her, because I didn't understand either.

So she sent me here. To the school counselor.

"The fight," I say.

"I remember. You told me about the fight with the astronauts, and the yelling. But why that fight in particular, Hannah? Why did it upset you so much?"

"Ambrose is unable to forget one single detail of his life," I say. A wet spot falls onto the paper. It mixes with some purple crayon. I smear the spot, and it looks like the Milky Way.

"What was that?" Ms. Meghan asks. She leans in toward me.

"It's from 'Lost in the Funhouse.' Ambrose can't

forget anything. That's what's wrong with him."

"You reread the passages?"

"I read them all the time," I admit.

"What can't you forget, Hannah?" Ms. Meghan urges.

If this were a story, I would be transformed into a stick of dynamite, lit and ready to explode with a secret I've been keeping for two years.

"Please, please don't make me, Ms. Meghan. Don't make me talk."

"I want to help you, Hannah. Let me help you." She puts her hand on my drawing.

I start with the first word. Talking feels like someone has struck the heaviness inside me with a pickax. The weight begins to break. I say the second word and feel even better. And then the truth spills out. The very worst day.

# The Very Worst Day

*I*f this were a story, this part would be a flashback, here to help you connect the dots, to help you understand why I cried in the line to music class and went to see Ms. Meghan and got the story "Lost in the Funhouse" and met Ambrose.

I lay on my stomach on the living room floor with a book in front of me. I kicked my feet against the ground like I was swimming through the hardwood.

"Can you stop that?" Dad asked from the couch. He put down his newspaper and took a sip of his drink. I stopped moving my legs.

I was reading a book about how to write stories. The chapter was on Freytag's triangle, which is a structure that helps stories stay on track. All the scenes in a story should fit into the triangle. I tried to apply my new knowledge to the show Mom was watching on TV. Mom liked shows about outer space. The astronauts on the screen were currently huddled around a monitor with worried looks on their faces. The captain

165

revealed that an asteroid was headed straight for the last planet with a known water source.

According to Freytag's triangle, this is the rising action. The place where the tension builds.

"I don't know why you watch this stuff," Dad said. Mom didn't answer. I peeked at her from under my eyelashes. She had her eyes fixed on the screen.

"Turn it down," he said. Mom was silent.

The astronauts started programming their laser and adjusting their position. They planned to blow the asteroid into a million pieces. This decision built up the action, which put them closer to the top of Freytag's triangle. The background music swelled.

"Did you hear me? I asked you to turn it down."

"I can hardly hear it as it is. Can you just deal with it?" Mom snapped back.

"What did you say?"

"I'm sick of walking on eggshells, Michael. I'm watching a show."

Dad stood up. I closed my book and hurried out of the way. The astronauts took aim at the asteroid.

"I don't know what eggshells you're referring to," Dad said.

"The ones you've laid all over this place," Mom

answered. She didn't look away from the TV. Dad stepped closer to Mom.

I knew which eggshells she was talking about. They had been scattered on the floor for as long as I could remember, crunching under our feet whenever the laundry was dirty or dinner was late or the day was too long.

The astronauts shot their laser. It hit the asteroid, but the giant rock didn't explode. The asteroid was laser resistant. The astronauts realized that their plan wouldn't work. Freytag's triangle calls this the climax. The most intense point of conflict.

"Say that again," Dad said.

"Day by day you're making this house unlivable," Mom said. Dad walked over to the TV and turned it off. Mom picked up the remote and turned it back on.

That's when Dad's arm reached back with his hand stretched out, positioned for a slap. Mom flinched. Dad didn't bring his arm back down. He kept it pulled back like a threat of what he was capable of. I ran from the room.

I don't know if the astronauts survived. The last part of Freytag's triangle is the resolution. There was none.

And there has never been any since.

# Counselor's Notes:
# Monday, November 2

**Name:** Hannah Geller

**Grade:** Five

**Reason for visit:** The issue with the notes is still unresolved. I hoped to engage with Hannah about the reason for her very first visit to the office, to see if issues at home are still affecting behavior.

**Demeanor:** She appeared stressed. Was willing to provide handwriting sample and pursue requested drawing activity. Drew a series of seemingly unrelated objects. Did so with a level of distress.

**Visit:** Admittedly, Hannah may have been pushed too hard during this visit. Relived a particularly painful argument between parents. I was aware of this argument but not to the extent described in this session. I have reason to believe that this is the first time that information of this nature was shared by Hannah.

**Next action:** Delay communication with parents. Continue to build trust. Argument happened two years ago. While it has impacted her mental state, she indicated that there have not been any similar episodes. Meet with Hannah again to assess what is happening in the present.

**Side note:** Someone please just give this girl a hug.

# Invisible Volcano

On the night before the spelling bee, it rains. I wait for the phone to ring. I worry Ms. Meghan will call and ask my parents about what I told her. I don't want to be around when it happens, so I tell Mom and Dad that I have homework and hide upstairs.

I sit at my desk by the window with my library book in front of me, watching the sky turn pink. Ambrose is in my lap.

"Maybe I shouldn't have told her," I say.

"You did the right thing," Ambrose reassures me.

"One word came out and then they all did. It felt good."

"Did you tell her that it's still happening?"

"It's not. That's the only time Dad almost hurt Mom." I turn the page of my book.

"If you say so, Hannah."

The phone rings. My pencil slips from my grasp to the ground. There's another ring, and then silence.

Someone has picked it up. I slide my hand into my lap, and it leaves a sweaty mark behind on the desk.

"Is it the school?" I ask Ambrose.

"Ohm." He makes a sound like a psychic looking into the future. "I got nothing."

It makes me laugh a little, since his speech is usually so formal.

"Thanks for trying."

Everything is completely still for another minute. Then the yelling starts.

"Did you forget to give me a message from John?" Dad asks in his loud voice.

"No, I wrote it in the notebook. It should be right there on the desk," Mom answers in her voice that tries to make a fight stop before it starts. It doesn't work.

From behind my door I can hear Dad search the desk, toss pieces of mail to the side, slam the drawer. Drop a cup full of paper clips to the floor. It sounds like an orchestra playing with out-of-tune instruments.

"It's not here, Jane. I had no idea he wanted to meet today. He plans to take his business elsewhere now. Are you happy?"

"Yes, Michael. I'm thrilled to death that you're losing business."

"How could you forget to tell me? It's the one thing I ask you to do, take the messages!"

"The same way you keep forgetting to fix the broken TV screen. How long could it possibly take to get a replacement?"

Hearing the argument through my closed door is like sensing an eruption from an invisible volcano. You don't know which way the lava is coming from, so you just run.

"I don't have the time, Jane. I mean, what are people going to think now? That I'm so unreliable, I can't respond to a simple message?" Dad questions.

"I'm sorry, okay. I'm sorry," Mom exclaims.

"That doesn't help now!"

"So stop using the house phone for clients! Stop bringing your work into this house every single day!"

I shake Ambrose.

"Do something," I plead.

"I can't," he says in a strained way.

"You're magic."

"It doesn't work like that, Hannah."

"Then just shut up!"

There's still yelling, so I go to my door and open it loudly enough for my parents to hear. That way they'll know I'm there and I'm listening. The fight pauses. I stay at the door. My parents and I wait in a silent standoff for someone to make a move.

"I'm going out for some air," Dad says. I hear the front door slam, and then his truck grumbles out of the driveway.

I lean my head against the wall.

"Go to sleep, Hannah," Mom calls out.

I close the door and sit with Ambrose again.

"I'm sorry for telling you to shut up."

He doesn't respond.

"Ambrose? Did you hear me?" I bang on the desk he sits on. His puffy gray body tips to the side, but he doesn't speak. I clutch him to my chest.

"Please don't leave." I let a tear fall onto his head and hope it might work like fairy dust to bring him back. Instead it soaks into his skin and disappears.

If this were a story, I would come home from school as though it were a normal day. I would take off my shoes and put my backpack away. Then I'd turn on the news and an anchorperson would announce that Ambrose the stuffed elephant has died, even though elephants should live for almost a hundred years.

I hold Ambrose in my arms and turn back to my book. Someone has torn the corner off page 125. I run my finger over the frayed edge and wonder why.

# From Hannah's Pages of "Lost in the Funhouse"

At this rate our protagonist will remain in the funhouse forever.

# The Spelling Bee

I take deep breaths in the bathroom stall on the day of the spelling bee finals. I'm thinking too much about the fight. My parents are somewhere in the gym ready to watch me compete. I wonder if the yelling is always with them, just waiting to burst out, like a snake that's grown too big for its skin. I think about disappearing.

"No. Not now. No," I say, and leave the stall. I remind myself that spelling is my happy place where everything can be okay if you take a minute to sound the problem out. Break it into syllables until it makes sense.

The bathroom door opens. I see Courtney standing there.

"Mrs. Bloom told me to come get you," she says, then walks into a stall and slams the door.

"I miss being your friend," I say before I can stop myself.

She doesn't answer.

I don't want to go, not while I have her here alone, but I also don't want to have a heart-to-heart through a stall door. I leave for the spelling bee.

The gym is turned into an auditorium full of folding chairs, like when we did *Romeo and Juliet*. The whole school is invited to come watch the spelling bee, and every grade has their own finals. I sit onstage with the other fifth-grade finalists, Kimmy and Rebecca. The bright lights above the stage are turned on, and I start to sweat from the heated glow. I can see far enough past the glare to find Ryan near the back, and another small hand waving in my direction. Ruby from Halloween grins at me. It warms me in a good way, and I brush my hair back from my face, ready to emerge *v-i-c-t-o-r-i-o-u-s*.

The school librarian, Mrs. Raymond, is our moderator again. I turn her opening speech into practice. We will *a-l-t-e-r-n-a-t-e* spelling words from the list. One wrong answer leads to *e-l-i-m-i-n-a-t-i-o-n*. We can ask for a *d-e-f-i-n-i-t-i-o-n* if we need it. The words will get increasingly *d-i-f-f-i-c-u-l-t*. Cheating is not *t-o-l-e-r-a-t-e-d*.

I clear my mind of everything but my brain

dictionary. I leave no room for the mean notes or the loss of Ambrose or the way Kimmy's eyes burn craters into the side of my skull.

The fifth-grade finals are last. Rebecca is called up and spells "gratification" correctly. Kimmy spells "delirious" before Mrs. Raymond even finishes saying the word. I take my place at the microphone.

"'Participant,'" Mrs. Raymond says.

"'Participant.' *P-a-r-t-i-c-i-p* . . ." I trail off. The word is simpler than a chocolate chip cookie, but I can't remember if it's an *e* or *a* before the *n-t*. My heartbeat is loud in my ears, a scary-day sound.

"You may start over one time if you need to." Mrs. Raymond looks at me over her glasses. I turn the pages in my brain dictionary so quickly, my thoughts practically get paper cuts.

"*A.*"

I look out into the hushed audience to see who shouted out the answer. No one looks back at me. No one else seems to have heard.

"*A.*" The voice sounds like it's coming from the curtains and the spotlights and the wooden floorboards. The stage is talking to me. Helping me, even though I didn't speak to him first. The way my magic works must be changing.

"'Participant.' *P-a-r-t-i-c-i-p-a-n-t*," I say.

"Correct." I sit back down in my chair and ignore the stage's whispers.

If this were a story, I would take the microphone into my hands and admit to having wires in my ears. I would tell everyone that a team of spies is outside in an unmarked van with a dictionary, feeding me the answers. Kimmy would win the bee and go all the way to nationals, and my punishment for cheating would be thirty seconds in a cage with a swarm of actual bees.

We go through three rounds before Rebecca spells "anthropomorphism" wrong. I'm avoiding my own anthropomorphism by spelling my words before the show-off stage can feed me the answers. Rebecca goes to sit back in the audience, and Kimmy walks up to the microphone. Her green shirt has been replaced by a white polo. Her hair is clean and tied into a tight ponytail. She has polished herself up to beat me.

"Spell 'metamorphosis.'"

Kimmy clears her throat.

"'Metamorphosis.' *M-e-t-a-m-o-r-p-h-a-s-i-s.*"

"I'm sorry, Kimmy. That is incorrect. Please take your seat."

I'm glad Kimmy is turned away from me, so I can't see if her face crumbles. She walks back to her chair with her head down.

"Hannah, if you can spell this word correctly, then you will represent Brookview at the citywide spelling bee. Spell 'introspection.'"

It isn't fair that I get this word. I know it better than the lines in my palm. It's the reason why, even on the verge of winning the spelling bee, I am thinking about Kimmy, about how her heart must be tearing in two, about how she must want to tear me in two. It's why at any given minute I can feel each drop of disappointment or pride or anger or joy that I've ever felt, as if it's happening right then, all over again.

"'Introspection.' *I-n-t-r-o-s-p-e-c-t-i—*"

"*O,*" the stage says.

*I know,* I say in my mind.

"Hannah?"

"*O-n.* 'Introspection.'"

"That's correct. You've won the school spelling bee. Congratulations."

The audience cheers with as much excitement as they can manage for a spelling bee. Ruby stands up in her chair to wave at me again. My parents clap their hands. They look proud.

"Thank you. Oh, thank you. You're too kind," the stage says, as if the audience were throwing roses at his feet.

I don't realize until now how long it's been since I had a moment without any weight pressing down on me. I feel full of bright lights and good words, like my whole body is smiling. I won.

We're supposed to meet in the library after the spelling bee for cookies and lemonade. The parents are invited too. I don't see Kimmy in the line on our way there. Courtney is ahead of me, consoling Rebecca. She whispers into Rebecca's ear and then looks over her shoulder at me. Some of the happiness in my heart leaks out like from a water balloon with a hole, but I manage to hold on to most of it.

*I won. I won. No one can take that from me.*

"Don't go to the library! Come here!" I hear from somewhere in the hallway. I recognize the voice, the way it's more of a scream. Penny. How did she get here?

I put my hand over my mouth.

"Where are you, Penny?" I whisper.

"Follow my voice! We'll play Hot or Cold!"

I see my parents through the glass walls outside the library. They stand with their arms crossed, close together but not talking. The sight of them pushes me out of line like real hands on my back.

"Where are you going?" Mrs. Bloom asks from behind me.

"Bathroom!" Penny shouts.

"Bathroom," I tell Mrs. Bloom.

"Quickly."

I walk fast down the hall and into the bathroom. I wait for Penny to guide me, but it's quiet.

"Penny?" I whisper.

"You're cold!" she answers. I step farther inside, toward the sinks.

"Warmer!"

I step again.

"Really warm!"

I'm in front of the sinks now. I look up into the mirror.

"You found me!"

"This is a mirror, Penny."

"You found me!

Tears burn in my eyes and make the blue in them turn so light, they're almost clear, like a window into all the sad things I think about. I use pieces of my hair to cover my face like a black curtain, so I can't see myself anymore.

"You're burning up!"

I shake my head and open my eyes to look through my hair. There's a green backpack on the floor. Penny must be talking about the bag, not the mirror. I know I shouldn't touch someone else's things, but I crouch down and move the backpack to look underneath.

A door flies open behind me, and Kimmy walks out of the stall.

"Get away from my stuff," Kimmy orders. She pulls the bag away from me and shoves what looks like a photo inside.

"I'm sorry. I was looking for something."

"You're such a freak. I heard you talking to yourself."

"I know. I'm sorry." My answer makes her look at me funny.

"Why did you have to beat me again, Hannah? I needed to make it to nationals. I'm good enough. And you still had to beat me." She puts her bag onto her shoulders.

"I'm sorry," I say again. It's like the vocabulary in my brain dictionary disappears, and all I'm left with are the apologizing words.

Kimmy clenches her jaw and goes for the door.

"And you better not try to blame me for what's in there."

"What?"

Kimmy points to the stall she came from, and walks out.

"Colder!" Penny screams before the door swings shut completely. She's muffled like she's shouting into a tunnel. Or from the inside of a backpack.

My arms and legs feel like they're buzzing when I open the stall door. There's writing on the wall ahead. A note on tile.

GO AWAY, HANNAH.

# Other Struggles

I don't go inside when I get home from school. Instead I go to the backyard and lie in the grass. The air is cool, but the sun is warm on my face. I keep my eyes closed until I hear someone sit next to me.

"It's a little chilly, isn't it?" Dad remarks.

"There's not much time left to lie outside. Winter is almost here."

"That's true." Dad lies down next to me. I turn my head to the side and take in his pine-tree smell. The newest bulletin from Mrs. Bloom is folded in Dad's hand.

"The police are talking to your class tomorrow?" he asks.

"Yeah. Mrs. Bloom thinks it will make us all really listen," I answer.

"It will, Hannah. Seeing an officer is going to make someone come forward. This will all be over soon."

"I hope so."

Dad reaches out and rubs my arm. I squeeze my eyes tight. His hand is the same one that builds houses and used to tuck me in and almost hurt Mom. How can I like and hate something so much at the same time?

"I love you, Hannah. And I'm so proud of you."

"I love you too, Dad."

I think that life is like one of those activity books. Some days are a crossword puzzle where you try to think of the right words. Others are a maze with one million dead ends.

"Want to help me set up the new TV?" Dad asks.

"Okay."

If this were a story, most of my days would be a match game, where you find pictures that go together. The picture of the astronauts matches with a scared Hannah. Lying with Dad in the backyard connects to a Hannah with hope.

Officer Riana stands in front of our classroom in full uniform. It's hard not to stare at the gun tucked into her belt. She clears her throat.

"Now, I know your teacher talked to you about this and so did your counselor. But it seems like the message hasn't quite gotten across." She eyes the pledge on the back wall.

Officer Riana's shiny brown ponytail swings when she paces in front of us. She holds her fingers in her belt loops.

"Bullying is serious. It's not cool or funny. It's not okay anywhere, and especially not at school."

The room is so quiet that her voice lingers after she's done speaking, like the rings that ripple out when a raindrop hits a puddle.

"I'm going to tell you why this needs to stop. Everyone close your eyes."

We all obey Officer Riana. At least I think we do. It's hard to say. My eyes are closed.

"Keeping your eyes closed, raise your hand if you're struggling with something right now. Your schoolwork or your friends or an activity. Anything."

I hesitate but raise my hand.

"Now open your eyes."

I open up to a classroom full of raised hands. Courtney and Rebecca and Theo and Katherine and

Joanie. Kimmy. Everyone has admitted to having hard things going on. Other struggles.

"Imagine if on top of that problem you're dealing with, you were also being bullied," Officer Riana says. I don't have to imagine too much. She's describing my story. The real one.

"It's also against the rules. That's why I'm here, because it's my job to stop the rules from being broken and people from getting hurt. Whoever did this, it's time to come forward. Because eventually we're going to find out."

Officer Riana looks toward Mrs. Bloom and nods. Mrs. Bloom walks her out. There's usually a moment after a guest speaker leaves when we all start chattering, getting our words out before class starts again. But not this time.

Mrs. Bloom looks exhausted when she gets back to the whiteboard, like she hasn't slept since someone started dropping notes in her classroom. I feel bad about that because she really is a nice teacher, who picks good books for us to read and buys ice cream sandwiches when we memorize our times tables.

"We were very close to canceling your pen pal field trip tomorrow," she says.

Everyone groans and gasps. Mrs. Bloom puts up her hand.

"We're still going, because it's important for you to visit the middle school. But if this bullying continues, there will be consequences. Now take out your math books."

I look at the first math problem on the page.

*If 4+A=7, what does A equal?*

*A* equals Ashley, and I get to meet her tomorrow. She won't know me as the girl who made the police come to school. I can just be her pen pal, the girl made of words.

# From Hannah's Pages of "Lost in the Funhouse"

"It is perfectly normal. We have
all been through it. It will not last
forever."

# Counselor's Notes:
## Wednesday, November 4

**Name:** Joanie Lawson

**Grade:** Five

**Reason for visit:** There was a mention of Joanie in a note collected by teacher about the bullying against Hannah Geller.

**Demeanor:** Joanie has nervous tendencies. Nail-biting, fidgeting, braid-twirling. Consistent with behavior from a session at the beginning of the school year, when she revealed an incident that had occurred over the summer during a movie night.

**Visit:** Transcript follows.

> COUNSELOR: How have things been, Joanie?
>
> STUDENT: The same, Ms. Meghan. Always the same.
>
> COUNSELOR: In what way?
>
> STUDENT: No one wants to forget about the movie. It's like I did the most hilarious and

disgusting thing anyone could ever do, and maybe I did, but it's getting really tiring to have to relive that stupid, embarrassing thing every single day.

COUNSELOR: Try to breathe, Joanie. A big, deep breath.

*Student takes a breath.*

COUNSELOR: I want the bullying to stop too.

STUDENT: Is that why I'm here?

COUNSELOR: It is. I want to help you. But I need your help too.

STUDENT: How can I help?

COUNSELOR: You could tell me anything you might know about the notes we talked about in your class. The notes about Hannah.

STUDENT: If you want to know about the notes, then talk to Courtney. She wrote them.

COUNSELOR: Courtney Gilmore? Isn't she a friend of Hannah's?

STUDENT: She's the meanest girl in this school. She's the one who won't let me or anyone else forget about the movie. She doesn't know how to be a friend.

COUNSELOR: It's going to pass, Joanie. I promise you.

STUDENT: Not with Courtney around.

**Next action:** As no one has come forward to claim responsibility for the notes, Brookview is planning a room search while the fifth-grade classes are on a field trip. We are hopeful that this will be the final step in determining the source of the notes, and bringing an end to the bullying in Mrs. Bloom's class.

# Pen Pals

It's the day of the pen pal field trip. We climb onto buses that will take us to the middle school, where we'll finally meet the eighth graders that we've been writing to since September. I wish I could sit next to Courtney or Ryan and tell them how my stomach turns over when I think about meeting Ashley. But Ryan is on a different bus, and Courtney sits three rows ahead of me with Rebecca.

I sit alone. Kimmy is behind me, kicking my seat hard with her boot. I ignore it, because it's partly my fault that she has so much hate. I told Ms. Meghan why I thought she wrote the notes. I beat her in the spelling bee. Now I'll pay for it with her foot in my back.

"Ouch," I say to an especially hard kick.

"Hullo?" I hear back. The voice is coming from my backpack. It speaks like it has its mouth full.

"Hi," I say. I look around to make sure no one is watching me. Kimmy keeps kicking.

"Where we off to?" Backpack asks.

"The middle school. I'm going to meet Ashley."

"What is she like?"

"Well, I know she dots her *I*s with little circles and that she likes to read magazines. And I know she's excited to meet me too. I hope she's nice."

"What if she's not?"

Backpack sounds too much like the scared thoughts running around inside my head.

"I don't want to talk to you anymore," I say, and Backpack goes quiet.

The bus stops in front of Prescott Middle School. I throw Backpack over my shoulders a little more roughly than I usually do, to teach him a lesson, but I feel bad about it afterward. I put so much weight inside him, no wonder he's a little grumpy.

Mrs. Bloom leads us through the front doors and down the hallway. Prescott Middle School smells like bleach and gym shoes and dusty carpets. There are lockers on the walls, sealed up by secret codes. I think about how "lockers," are designed to keep people out. Maybe when I go to middle school next year and get assigned my own locker, I will break the lock right off.

We walk into the eighth-grade classroom, and suddenly I'm looking at a million different combinations of freckles and glasses and haircuts. I have no idea which combination makes up Ashley, and that makes me so nervous that I have to take a big breath.

"Welcome, welcome. We're so thrilled to meet you," the other teacher, Mr. Barnes, announces. The class doesn't look too thrilled. Their teacher calls their names, and one by one we're paired off. Courtney goes to sit with her pen pal, Shelby, who has streaks of blue dye in her hair and holes in her jeans.

"Hannah, come meet Ashley," Mr. Barnes says, and then I'm finally seeing Ashley, the girl I wrote so neatly for so that she would know how much I cared about our pen-pal-ship. Ashley smiles at me. She wears pink lipstick and waves me over like she's excited. When I sit down next to her, I can see that she has swollen red bumps on her forehead and cheeks. Like me, only her pimples are covered with orange makeup.

"Nice to meet you, girl," Ashley says, and shakes my hand.

"Do you need my gloves?" I ask her. She squints a little, and I can see the brown shimmer on her lids. It matches the color of her eyes.

"Why?"

"Your hands are cold."

Ashley laughs, and it sounds like how I think twinkling stars would sound.

"You're so sweet. I'm okay, though. Thanks."

Mrs. Bloom and the other teacher start passing out balls of aluminum foil and plastic knives. I stare at our round package.

"Inside the aluminum foil are owl pellets," Mrs. Bloom says. "You're going to dissect these pellets and report your findings with your pen pal."

The data collection sheets are passed down the rows of desks. Ashley hands one to me. Her nail polish is chipped and blue.

"This could be very enlightening," I whisper.

"You do like words, don't you?" she replies.

"Love them."

"'Enlightening' is a good one. The dissection could also be illuminating."

"Which means that something becomes clear," I

say. She winks at me, and I smile so hard, my cheeks hurt.

Mrs. Bloom and the other teacher tell us to unwrap our pellets and start using the knife to dig. They instruct us to document what we see inside the pellet.

"Go ahead. You do it," Ashley says. I pull up my sleeves and unwrap the aluminum foil. The pellet looks like a chunk of earth. I pick up the knife and stab at the surface. It crumbles under the blade.

I move the pieces of the pellet around and find bones inside. I dig harder and free a tiny mouse skull from its pellet prison. It is still whole and unbroken and is the color of old paper.

"Ashley's like you. And if she's okay, then you'll be okay too," the mouse skull squeaks to me.

I'd like to tell the mouse skull that I agree, but I can't talk to it in front of Ashley. I've completely lost control of my magic, which is short-circuiting like a hair dryer that fell in water.

I drop the knife.

"Do you want to try?" I ask. Ashley is looking across the room toward Shelby and Courtney.

Courtney is holding her nose and poking at the pellet. Shelby turns toward us and nods her head.

"That's okay, Hannah. You know what could be fun? Let's go to the bathroom, and I'll put some makeup on you. I can show you how to cover those pimples right up," Ashley says.

I hope one day if I'm a pen pal, I'll have some useful advice to share. Like how to use makeup, or how to spell words that seem impossible. I nod to Ashley, and she gets up to take a bathroom pass from her teacher. We walk together down the hallway. I notice when we pass two bathrooms without stopping.

"Weren't we going to the bathroom?" I ask.

"We're meeting Shelby outside first," she answers.

"Outside? Are we allowed?"

"We aren't leaving school property."

I think Ashley wants me to be grown-up like she is, so I follow. She leads us out the back doors of the school and into the parking lot. I have no jacket, and the November chill easily seeps through my sweater.

A minute later, Shelby and Courtney make it to the parking lot. We walk down a hill to the baseball field, ending up in the far dugout. The bench is coated in dust. I brush it away with my hand and make enough clean space for Courtney. She looks back and forth between Shelby and me but doesn't sit.

Shelby reaches into her purse and pulls out two cigarettes. She hands one to Ashley. Ashley puts the cigarette into her mouth and lets Shelby light it for her, her hand cupped around the flame to block the wind.

"You girls want to share one?" Ashley asks.

Courtney's eyes go wide, and she scatters across the cement floor of the dugout to sit next to me. Having her back, even for a second, is like a bonfire to warm me from the cold truth about Ashley.

"We're ten," I say.

"So? I had my first cigarette at ten."

"Why?"

"That's a silly question, Hannah." Smoke slips out of Ashley's lips when she laughs. She leaves a lipstick mark on the end of the cigarette. It becomes clear that Ashley's niceness toward me was just like makeup, concealing the problems under the surface.

Since she won't answer my question, I start trying to answer it for myself. What would make a girl smoke when she's ten?

Courtney nudges me with her elbow.

"I know you were excited to meet her," she says. It's good to hear her voice, and know that I'm tucked somewhere in her mind even when we're not speaking to each other.

"I'm still excited," I say.

Courtney shakes her head. "I wish I looked at things the way you do."

"What do you mean?"

"I don't know. It's like you think about things from every angle."

I consider that. It's easy to find the sad details of everything that happens. I'm a professional at that. But I do try my best to find the good, too.

"Maybe that's true," I say.

"I made it seem like that was a bad thing, but really, it's why you're such a good friend. I'm not. I should have been there for you through the notes like you were there for me with . . ." She trails off. I hold up my hand.

"Are you here now?" She smiles, and her pink glasses climb up the bridge of her nose.

"Definitely." She touches my palm with hers. Our hands make a friendship prayer.

"What's going on over there?" Ashley asks. She crushes the cigarette into the wall of the dugout, and the burning end is extinguished.

I test the new theory of my thought process on Ashley. She's not who I thought she would be. She's not Madonna, or a girl from the seventies, or the sister I never had. But maybe it's not fair for me to wish she were someone different. I can find the good in my pen pal exactly the way she is.

"We don't want to get in trouble," Courtney says, and stands up.

"All right. Let's get you inside." Shelby pulls a bottle of cucumber-melon body spray from her purse and drenches herself in it before passing it to Ashley. Ashley walks over to us and starts spraying.

"We didn't smoke," I say.

"Secondhand smoke smells just as much." She sprays us a few more times and then puts the bottle back into Shelby's purse. Our time in the dugout is masked in the fruity scent.

Courtney and I walk side by side behind our pen pals back into the school.

"You have to stop being mean to people, Courtney," I tell her. I didn't know until now how much I needed to say that. She nods.

"I know."

"It's not who you're supposed to be."

"It's not who I want to be either."

I hope that she means it. I hope that she'll leave her bully bones buried at the baseball field. We link arms the rest of the way to the classroom.

"Awful long bathroom break, girls," Mr. Barnes says when we make it back.

"Girl problems, Mr. Barnes," Ashley says in front of the whole class, and her teacher turns red.

I sit with Ashley in front of our dissected pellet. She picks up a plastic knife and moves the pieces around. Her eyes look sleepy.

"I figured it out," I say.

"Figured what out?"

"Why you smoke."

She hisses a *shh* at me and looks around the room. "What are you talking about?"

"You do it because you know you shouldn't. You

hope it might help someone notice that you're not okay." Ashley points the plastic knife at me, her jaw clenched tight. I back away.

"Look, you might think you're smart because of your big words, but you have no idea what you're talking about."

She starts scribbling on our data collection sheet with her big, bubbly letters. She writes about the bones we found inside the pellet, and lies about the ones we didn't. She forgets about the little mouse skull entirely.

"There. We're done," she announces.

When everyone's finished digging, we walk around the room to look at other people's pellets.

If this were a story, the desks would turn into tombstones. Instead of writing on data collection sheets, we would carve the names of the bones we found into the granite. *Here lies rat femur. Here lies shrew rib.* Fog would roll in from the windows, and we'd leave flowers on the graves.

It's hard to keep my feet moving. I catch Ashley's eye a few times from across the room, but she looks away quickly. It hurts when something ends and all you have left are the bony remains.

• • •

We get off the bus that afternoon and walk in a line to our classroom. Courtney is ahead of me. She taps Joanie on the shoulder.

"I'm sorry, Joanie," Courtney says. Joanie's eyes wander the hallway like there's a practical joke waiting for her around the corner.

"Really?" she asks.

"I mean it. I won't bring up what happened anymore."

"How am I supposed to believe you?" She twists a bright red braid around her finger.

Courtney looks up and down the line and then cups her hands around her mouth.

"Hey, everyone, remember when I threw up all over John Block?" she announces.

Some people start laughing, but it's not mean laughing, and Courtney joins in. It's like that horrible moment has turned into a funny memory we all share instead. Joanie smiles bigger than I've seen her do all school year.

"Shh, shh. Too loud, everyone," Mrs. Bloom says, but we're all laughing too hard to stop.

We get close to our classroom door and see Ms. Meghan waiting just outside. I see her eyes shift between Courtney, Joanie, and me. They settle on me. She talks quickly with Mrs. Bloom, and then Mrs. Bloom opens the door to let us inside. I look straight ahead, determined to stroll into the classroom and sit at my desk and get through the rest of the school year with my best friend back the way she used to be. Ms. Meghan touches my shoulder when I try to pass.

"Can you come with me, Hannah?"

I step out of line with shaky legs.

"We have your parents in the conference room," Ms. Meghan says when the class finishes shuffling into the room.

"Why?"

"We did a search of the classroom while you were all gone, and we found some things in your desk. Pieces of notebook paper with torn corners. Handwriting samples that match what was on the notes."

My breath comes in short, heavy bursts.

"You think I did it?" I ask.

"We're not blaming you for anything. We'd just

206

like to talk." She stretches her arm out toward the hallway, toward where my parents are waiting for me.

If this were a story, then this would be the part where the main character tries to see the good in the situation but comes up empty.

# Conference

My parents are at a circular table with Principal Jenkins. The notes lie on the table, along with torn pieces of paper from my desk and the drawing I did in Ms. Meghan's office. There's a picture of the writing on the bathroom wall, too. The papers form a line between us and the staff. Gellers vs. Brookview.

"Sit down, Hannah." Principal Jenkins points to the chair between my parents. Dad's mouth is in a hard line when he watches me cross the room. Mom touches my leg when I sit down. A vent pours out so much artificial heat that I have to put a cold hand to my face.

If this were a story, Gellers vs. Brookview would take place in a courtroom. Principal Jenkins would wear a white wig, and my parents would sit on a wooden bench. Ms. Meghan would instruct me to put my hand on a Bible and tell only the truth. Suddenly the Bible would turn into a bird and snatch the gavel from Principal Jenkins, before flying over to me. "Hold on," the bird would say to me. I'd grab its wing and soar through the windows without getting cut by the glass. The bird would drop me off on a deserted island and then fly back into the sky, joining a long *V* of other birds on their way to Florida.

"The most important thing for you to know is that you're not in any trouble. We want to have an honest conversation. We hope you will be honest," Ms. Meghan says and sits across from me.

"About what?"

"Did you write these notes, Hannah?"

"I didn't write them," I say. Ms. Meghan half-smiles.

"There you go. If she said she didn't do it, she didn't do it," Dad says. His hand is in a fist on the table, next to the first note. NOBODY LIKES HANNAH.

"Hannah is the only one who had torn paper like this in her desk," Principal Jenkins says. "You can see from the drawing that her name is written very similarly to the handwriting on the notes and the bathroom wall." I want to flip the table over.

"She's a good girl. There has to be some sort of explanation," Mom adds. The mousse in her bun isn't working; the flyaways are flying everywhere. She grips my leg more tightly. It might've hurt a little if my limbs didn't feel all injected with that numbing medicine they use at the dentist.

"Can you give us that, Hannah? Can you give us an explanation?" Ms. Meghan asks.

My magic has a mind of its own now, but I try to find something, anything, in the room to talk to me. I focus on Ms. Meghan's coffee mug. It's white with a tie-dyed peace sign printed on it.

*Help,* I say to the mug with my mind.

"What do you want me to do, tip over? That's a serious shattering hazard, and I'm really jittery," the mug answers.

*Tell me what to say.*

"Hannah?" Ms. Meghan urges.

"Tell them you write notes to your friends," the mug offers.

"I write notes to my friends sometimes. Just normal notes. I know we're not supposed to, but that's why I have the ripped paper."

"And what about the handwriting?" Principal Jenkins asks.

*Mug?* I channel.

"Idon'tknow,Hannah. Ijustdon'tknow," the mug rants. His words run together like a train wreck. A little steam pours out of his top.

*Calm down, Mug.*

I'm on my own.

"I can't explain the similarities. All I can tell you is that I didn't write them," I say.

"We want to believe you," Ms. Meghan responds.

"Then believe her," Dad retorts.

"Someone needs to be suspended for this, and we have the most cause to suspect Hannah," Principal Jenkins says. "We can give her only so much benefit of the doubt."

"Maybe we can spend some time talking about Hannah's home life," Ms. Meghan suggests.

"What does she mean by that?" Mug asks. I ignore him.

Dad stands up so fast, his chair nearly tips over.

"I won't let you pin this on her just because it's convenient." Dad rests a hand on my shoulder. Half of me wants to collapse into him, and the other half wants to run, but both halves are just so tired.

Principal Jenkins calls an end to the meeting and tells me I can go back to class. My parents start walking me out of the office.

"What about the home life, Hannah? What about the home life? Are you okay?" Mug calls out to me.

The door closes behind us before I can answer.

# Here's What Happened to the Astronauts

Captain Bass held his breath and watched the red line of the laser make contact with the asteroid. The targeted planet hung in the distance like a dartboard waiting to be struck.

"Sir? The asteroid is absorbing the laser." Jessica turned to face him from the window of their shuttle. Her face was softer than a second-in-command's should be.

The laser's light grew heavier and darker as it dug into the side of the asteroid. It burned and burned at the point of contact and then exploded into crimson flames. The crew's shuttle rocked back and forth from the impact. There wasn't even a small crater left in the surface of the asteroid.

"Was that the last blast?" Captain Bass asked.

"It doesn't matter. The thing's laser resistant," Brainy Jack said from behind his computer.

"What else can we do?"

The crew offered their suggestions:

"Bombs?"

"Freeze Spray?"

"Fire Cannon?"

"We don't have time to experiment. None of those are stronger than the laser," Captain Bass said. To try to find a hidden solution, he thought about his last five years as a captain. He and his crew had saved the universe in impossible ways at the very last minute so many times before. There had to be a way.

The space shuttle flew parallel to the asteroid, keeping speed with it. The targeted planet grew larger in the windows. It was close enough for the crew to see the lakes that covered the surface, the rivers that ran through the mountains like paths of tears.

Jessica cleared her throat.

"That planet is the last one in the universe with water. If the asteroid hits, everyone we know will eventually die. We'll die too."

"Was there an idea in there? 'Cause I'm pretty sure we already know that," Brainy Jack said.

"What are you thinking, Jessica?" Captain Bass asked. He looked at Jessica. Her eyes were as blue as that doomed planet.

"It can be the whole world that dies, or it can just be us."

"You're saying . . ."

"We need to give the asteroid a new target. We need to sacrifice ourselves."

The crew chimed in with their disagreement. Captain Bass held up his hand. The planet was all they could see from the windows now. The rest of the star-studded sky had disappeared.

"She's right."

He took his place in the captain's chair and put his hand on the controls. The crew got into position. The space shuttle dipped and redirected itself into the asteroid's path, where it would strike them instead of the planet. The planet disappeared from sight and was replaced by the rocky surface of the asteroid. Jessica reached out from her chair to hold Captain Bass's hand.

"Crew, don't you ever forget. We always save the day," Captain Bass declared.

Then the TV screen went black.

No one knows for sure if the astronauts perished or survived. The TV show got canceled.

# Have a Happy Day, Brookview Elementary

I should be walking to school, but instead I'm frozen at my front door. It's only a matter of time before they decide whether to blame me for the notes.

If this were a story, I would be an accused criminal in medieval times. Today would be the day I face the guillotine, a crowd gathering in the town square to turn my sentencing into a spectacle.

Thank goodness this isn't a story. Being suspended would be a catastrophe, but I definitely don't want my head chopped off.

"What are you doing?" Dad asks from the kitchen table.

"Waiting. It's early," I say. He stands up from his bowl of cereal and joins me at the door. He puts an arm around my shoulder. I want to cry for a million reasons and no reason at all.

"This past month must have been hard." Dad looks out the front door. When the notes started, there were still leaves on the trees. So much has changed. I can't recognize the bare skeletons the fall has left behind, or the reflection of myself in the glass.

"I'm okay."

"Maybe we should change schools. Brookview hasn't taken good enough care of you."

I hear Mom moving around in the kitchen, picking up Dad's bowl from the table.

"But my friends are there. And I'm the spelling bee champion."

"Is that what's most important?"

"I don't know."

On that day, the worst day, Mom said she was tired of walking on eggshells. I'm tired of it too, but I just can't make myself stomp down. What will happen to all those little broken pieces? I pull away and open the door. The cold air hits me like a painful memory.

"We'll talk about this later," Dad says.

I nod at him and run away from another chance to speak up.

• • •

Courtney sits at our blue caterpillar (I mean "table") again. There's not enough room inside me for the gladness that she's back. Nerves stab my stomach like spikes from a cactus.

"Are they going to suspend you?" Courtney asks.

"They can't. You didn't do it," Ryan says, and pulls the chips from Courtney's lunch bag.

"Innocent people get sent to jail all the time." Courtney takes Ryan's banana in retaliation.

"Thanks for that," I say.

If today were normal, if I were normal, I'd join in the food war. I'd steal Courtney's sandwich and Ryan's carrots. I wouldn't feel like a nighttime sky with no moon or stars to break up all the darkness.

The cafeteria sounds blend together and attack my ears. The chatter is like metal scraping metal. The footsteps are like firing cannonballs. A scream builds up inside me.

"I'm going to the bathroom," I tell my laughing friends.

"We're just kidding, Hannah," Courtney says.

"Don't be mad," Ryan says.

"I'm not mad! I'm not anything!"

*Liar.*

I retreat from their worried eyes.

Bubby the lunch monitor writes me a pass and lets me go. I don't look back.

I make it to the bathroom and sit down in a stall with my head in my hands. *Just shut up for one minute*, I tell my head. *Just for one single minute stop thinking.* I slow down my breathing and clench the hall pass, willing each breath to bring some kind of calm over me.

"Have a happy day, Brookview Elementary."

The pass slips from my hand.

The code words.

The lockdown code words.

This can't be a drill. Bubby never would have let me leave the cafeteria if he'd known there was going to be a drill.

If this were a story, then—no, no, no. This isn't a story!

I'm not ready for my life to have a climax. I should be in the cafeteria, with Ryan on one side of me and Courtney on the other. Instead I'm surrounded by walls that don't even reach the ground, that don't even have a ceiling, that don't hide me from any angle. There are empty spaces all over the stall, and still it's closing in on me.

I am Ambrose. I am lost in the funhouse. I am alone.

# Alone

I curl myself into a ball on the toilet seat until I'm as small as possible, and I wait. All the sadness from the notes comes crashing down over me. *Nobody likes Hannah. Why would anyone be friends with Hannah? Go away, Hannah.* The words can't be real, they just can't be.

My legs shake from balancing. I don't know how much longer I can do this. The thick smell of flowery soap makes my head spin. A small sob escapes my throat, and I throw my hand over my mouth before I'm found.

"Hello?" I hear.

I freeze. I don't know what's speaking to me.

"Who's talking?" I whisper. I put my ear to the toilet paper dispenser. "Is it you?"

"I'm a girl," the voice says. It's coming from the stall next to me. I want to stand up and look over the top of the wall to see who I'm trapped with, but I can't. We're still in hiding.

"Do you know what's happening?" I ask, trying to keep my voice as quiet as I can.

"No, I've been in here a long time," she says.

"How long?"

"Since October."

I feel a teardrop on my cheek. The girl in the stall next to me makes no sense. But she's all I have.

"I've felt a little trapped too," I say.

"Why?" the voice asks.

I take a deep but quiet breath.

"There were these notes on my classroom floor. They were hurtful. It all turned into a big mess, and now everyone just wants to know who wrote them."

"Who did write them?"

"Why do you assume I know?"

"I'm not assuming. I'm just scared."

I put a hand on the wall that separates me from the girl on the other side, as if it might comfort her. All the things I've held on to for so long don't seem so important. I've turned myself into a locker. If I ever get out, I'll release my memories into the air like dandelion seeds and watch them fly away.

"Have you ever read 'Lost in the Funhouse'?" I ask.

"No."

"There's a character named Ambrose, and he has a lot going on in his head. He has all these bad memories and this self-consciousness, and he just doesn't feel normal. And the worst part is that he doesn't know how to tell anyone what's wrong."

"What does that have to do with the notes?" the girl asks.

"I just think if someone couldn't talk about their thoughts, they might end up doing something, well, crazy. They might become a bully."

"How does the story end?"

When I think about "Lost in the Funhouse," I never think about the last passage in the stack. It takes me a minute to answer.

"He decides he's going to build funhouses for other people like him. Places where they can't get lost."

"Is that what you're going to do?" the girl asks.

"What do you mean?"

"You're Ambrose, aren't you?"

By only thinking of Ambrose as lost, I've been taking away his conclusion this whole time. I forgot about the moment when he realizes the good he can do. Maybe I've been taking my resolution away too. It would be worth it to be the way I am if I could help other people. People like Ruby or Ashley or maybe even the girl from the arcade.

"Yeah. That's what I'm going to do."

The door to the bathroom bursts open so hard, it smacks the wall. My heart jump-starts, and I clutch my knees even tighter into my chest. I close my eyes and mumble apologies to everyone: to my parents, to Kimmy, to Ms. Meghan. To myself.

"Hannah? Hannah, are you in here?" I hear.

"Bubby?"

"Yes, yes, it's me. You're safe; you can come out." I want to run from the stall, but instead I stand slowly and peek through the cracks. I see Bubby's gray hair and white T-shirt. I'm crying when I open the door and finally walk out of my little box. Bubby wraps his arm around my shoulders while they shake.

"Was it a drill?" I ask.

"Not this time. Are you all right?" he asks. Before I can ask what happened, I remember that I wasn't alone.

"There's someone else in here." I walk up to the stall next to mine and knock. "We're safe now. Come out." No sound comes out of the stall. No feet finally climb off the toilet.

"Really, it's okay, come out," I try again. Still nothing. "Come on!" I push the door, and it flies open.

The stall is empty. There's no girl hiding inside. A fresh patch of paint covers the place where the writing on the wall used to be.

Bubby clears his throat behind me. "That's all right, Hannah. Let's get you out of here."

In stories there are moments called revelations. I think I'm having mine. Maybe I do have magic inside me, but it's not the type that brings stuffed animals and objects to life. It was just me all along, leading myself to where I am now, showing me what I have to do.

I don't know what danger is out in the halls, but I'm running. Away from the bathroom. Away from the thoughts that tell me to stop. All the way to Ms. Meghan's office.

She is typing furiously at her computer.

"Ms. Meghan?" I say. She looks up at me with a moon-white face.

"Hannah?"

"I have to talk to you about the notes," I say.

"Hannah, we don't have to talk about that right now. There's just been a situation," Ms. Meghan says.

"Please, I have to. I have to tell the truth."

"What is it?"

I take a deep breath. I blow out the part of me that keeps everything in, that can't talk about how I feel, that would rather write painful notes about the thoughts piled up in my head than just say the words out loud.

"I did it. I wrote them."

# From Hannah's Pages of "Lost in the Funhouse"

For all a person knows the first time through, the end could be just around any corner; perhaps, *not impossibly* it's been within reach any number of times.

# Confession

I wait with Ms. Meghan in the office for my parents. Officer Riana walks in with her sights set on Principal Jenkins's door. I know she's not here for me. My crime has been overshadowed by whatever sent the school into lockdown. Ms. Meghan won't tell me anything about it.

"I'm proud of you, Hannah," Ms. Meghan says. I'm surprised enough to look away from the door.

"Proud?" I ask.

"I can only imagine how hard it must have been for you to tell the truth." One police officer comes out of the office. Then a second one. I can't see until they're close to the door, but there is someone walking between them with her head down, tears streaming down her cheeks. Kimmy.

Like so many other times, the first thing I think about is "Lost in the Funhouse."

If you knew all the stories behind all

the people on the boardwalk, you'd see
that *nothing* was what it looked like.


I turn back to Ms. Meghan.

"I think it will be easier to tell the truth now,"
I say.

"Are you ready to test that out?" she asks, and
nods her head toward the door. Mom and Dad are
walking through.

"Yes. I'm ready."


I sit on the living room couch with my parents in
front of me. Their faces are wrinkled like bewildered
raisins. Dad looks at the ground as if something has
died. My heart aches because I disappointed them,
but it aches even more to finally tell them why.

"I'm sorry," I start. This only melts the ice in their
eyes a little bit.

"Why, Hannah? You had so many chances to tell
the truth. Why would you do something like this at
all?" Mom says.

"I needed . . . attention." It's not a good enough
explanation. It sounds like a tantrum.

"This is how you want to get attention? By bullying yourself?" Mom continues.

"When you were worried about me, you stopped fighting. I just wanted to stop the fighting. You never talk to each other anymore. You just yell." My parents sit next to me on the couch.

"You couldn't tell us that?" Dad asks.

"It's hard for me to say how I feel. It's easier to keep it all locked up inside."

"Adults fight, Hannah. Everyone who loves each other fights," Mom says.

I take a breath. I have to say the hardest words, the ones that hurt the most.

"So much that they almost hit each other?" I ask.

Dad makes a sound in his throat like a sob that got stuck.

"I never should have done that, Hannah. I've made a lot of mistakes, and put you through too much. Both of you." Dad's cheeks are red, but not the angry red, the rosy red that comes from crying. I have never seen him cry. It makes me feel embarrassed, because I did this.

"Don't cry, Daddy." He pulls me in close. Mom

wraps me up from the other side, and the three of us stay that way for a long time.

"I want us to be happy," I whisper into our tangled-up hug.

"We will be. You'll see," Dad replies. From my place between my parents, I see him look at Mom. "No more taking work out on you. Nothing is more important than home."

Mom smiles with watery eyes.

Dad mumbles "I'm so sorry" a few more times, and then we are quiet.

"Am I still in trouble?" I ask when the hug ends.

"Oh yeah," my parents say together.

Mom takes the bun out of her hair and reties it. It looks perfect.

Sunlight gathers on the windowpane, the one that looks to the backyard. The grass still slopes the same way. The trees are the same ones that have grown beside me. But I feel in my healing heart that now my family will be different.

# Counselor's Notes:
# Friday, November 6

**Name:** Kimmy Dobson

**Grade:** Five

**Reason for visit:** Kimmy visited several empty classrooms and stole money, expensive clothing, and cell phones. Did so while wearing a Frankenstein mask. Dropped a backpack in the hallway. This was seen on the security cameras and prompted a lockdown. She proceeded to run out of the school and hide in the woods when lockdown was announced.

**Demeanor:** Kimmy was extremely distraught. Expressed significant regret over decision. Was inconsolable to the point of physical sickness. Unresponsive to conversation for several minutes before settling down enough to talk.

**Visit:** Transcript follows.

> COUNSELOR: Kimmy, please, settle down and talk to me. We're just talking.
>
> STUDENT: I'm so sorry, I'm so sorry, I'm so sorry.

COUNSELOR: I know you are. Why were you stealing?

STUDENT: I thought I was going to go to the national spelling bee. I thought I would win the prize money. But then I lost. I just wanted to help my grandma. Oh, Grandma, I'm so sorry!

COUNSELOR: Your grandma loves you, Kimmy. She begged to take care of you when your mom died. Do you remember?

STUDENT: She won't love me now. No one is ever going to love me again.

COUNSELOR: That's not true. You are always going to be more than the mistakes you make. This is going to pass.

STUDENT: I swear I was going to give everything back. I don't know what I was thinking. I couldn't really steal.

COUNSELOR: Is that why you left the bag behind in the hallway?

STUDENT: Yes. I just wanted to give it all back before anyone could know it was me. I wasn't thinking, I wasn't thinking at all.

COUNSELOR: I believe you, Kimmy.

STUDENT: You do?

COUNSELOR: Yes.

STUDENT: Am I suspended?

**Next action:** School will suspend Kimmy for action. I can tell that she is sincerely apologetic. This action was a buildup of extreme emotion that she could not get a handle on. Kimmy will meet regularly with therapist before being readmitted to school. I hope that a fresh start will be waiting for her when she returns.

# Life Goes On

I'm grounded for two weeks, the length of my suspension. I spend the time reading and thinking about my powers. Ambrose sits on the bed with me, but I don't try to wake him up. I still believe there's magic in sounds, but it doesn't come from pennies or stop signs or coffee mugs. The magic comes from listening to yourself.

Two days before my suspension and groundedness ends, my parents decide I can go to the park with Courtney. We sit on the seesaw and push ourselves up and down.

"Ryan and I miss you," Courtney says. I jump, and my feet are lifted into the air.

"I miss you both too. Who got to be spelling bee champion?"

"Rebecca."

Losing my place in the citywide spelling bee was one of the worst parts of my punishment. It felt like dropping back down to the ground on a seesaw; your stomach gets left at the top.

"Does everyone know what happened?" I ask.

"You were officially overshadowed by Kimmy."

"Why do you think she did it?"

"Why did you write the notes? Why does anyone do anything?" We seesaw in silence for a minute.

"It's those other struggles that Officer Riana told us about. Everyone's hurting from something."

Courtney hops off the seesaw and picks up her pink purse. She pulls out a plastic bag and then one of the rolls of pennies.

"Let's do something about that, then."

We climb on top of platforms and crawl in the grass, even though our clothes get muddy. Anything to plant the heads-up pennies without being seen. I'm preparing to put one inside the tire swing, when I see someone sitting under the oak tree, headphones in her ears. The wind blows her green checkered shirt. I keep the penny in my hand and start to walk over to her.

"Hannah, no. Are you crazy?" Courtney comes up behind me. She looks around and then places a penny on the ground by our feet.

"She's alone," I say.

I leave Courtney behind and cross the open field to the oak tree. Kimmy doesn't hear me when I approach.

"Hey," I say. She looks up and pulls the headphones out of her ears before standing. She takes a step toward me but then retreats, like for a second she can't remember why she's supposed to hate me.

"Hi," she says.

"I'm sorry you got suspended."

If this were a story, a spontaneous hurricane would break out across the park. The kind that rips up trees and knocks down the playground and sucks cars up into the wind with passengers still inside. Then, all of a sudden, it would just stop. Life would go on.

"Me too," Kimmy answers.

"And I'm sorry if I had anything to do with what you did. I shouldn't have blamed you for the notes."

Kimmy digs a hole in the ground with her boot.

"I think it would've happened anyway. I think I wanted other people to feel just as hurt as I was. But it was a mistake, and I regretted it right away."

"I know what you mean."

Her cheeks turn a shy kind of red.

"I did write one note about you," she says.

"You did?"

"During the kind words activity. The one that said you were a good person."

Maybe it is true that one kind act can fix everything.

"I wrote that you were a good speller," I admit.

"That is so true."

I laugh and reach into my pocket for a roll of pennies. I hold them out to her. "Do you want to come spread some good luck with us?"

Kimmy smiles, and her face breaks open like she was wearing a mask this whole time. She is unrecognizable when she reaches into her backpack for a tattered coin purse.

"I have my own."

We meet back up with Courtney, who explains the rules of coin-dropping to Kimmy. Then we run together through the park, three friends on a mission.

In "Lost in the Funhouse" Ambrose wishes he had someone in the funhouse with him. The two could work together to get out of the dark, learning about each other and themselves along the way. When they

finally made it out of the funhouse and into the sunlight, he would see that the friend he'd made in his
darkest minutes was not who he had expected. It
might even be his enemy.

"Where should we put this one?" Kimmy asks.
She lifts a penny from her coin purse. It looks like
every other penny on the face of this earth, but I know
it's her. Penny. She was with Kimmy this whole time.

"Let's put her on top of the tower," I suggest.

"Her?" Courtney asks.

I run away from the question, and Kimmy and
Courtney follow. We put Penny at the highest point of
the wooden tower.

"How's this?" Kimmy asks.

"Perfect!" I shout in a Penny voice.

Penny can see everything from here. She can see
the trees and the grass and the swirl of blue-gray sky.
I hope she can see that everyone is going to be okay.

# Last Letter

The morning before my suspension ends, Ms. Meghan comes to see me at home.

"Can we talk for a minute? I have something for you." She pulls a white envelope from her coat pocket. My name is written on the outside. I put a jacket on over my pajamas and sit with Ms. Meghan on the front steps.

"What is it?" I ask her.

"It's a letter from your pen pal. I thought you might like to read it." She hands the envelope to me. I must not look as happy as she expected, because she asks, "What's wrong?"

"The funhouse in the story wasn't really a funhouse, was it? It was life. Ambrose was lost in life."

Ms. Meghan looks out into the distance.

"I'd say that's up to the reader. But I would agree that the funhouse was Ambrose's life."

"I think he found his way."

"I think so too."

We sit in silence for a moment.

"Do you remember Riley Jones?" I ask.

"Of course. Why?"

"I was thinking we could plant flowers around his tree. In the spring, when its warm again. I want him to know that we still remember."

Ms. Meghan leans her head against her palm and looks at me with soft, puzzled eyes. I think she's getting used to the way my mind connects things, how a letter from my pen pal can lead to revelations about "Lost in the Funhouse" and flowers for Riley Jones.

"That's a great idea. I'll see you soon, Hannah," she says.

When Ms. Meghan leaves, I take my letter to the hill in my backyard and sit in the grass. With shaky hands I tear the envelope open and start to read.

Dear Hannah,
I'm sorry I wasn't the pen pal you
expected. I can honestly tell you that
I didn't mean to be a disappointment.
Being thirteen is a lot like being ten. It's
confusing. It seems like the more you get

to know about yourself, the harder it is to be that person. You start to wish you could be someone else. And then things get messy. You were right about what you said. I don't know how you figured me out so quickly.

You're different, Hannah. I can tell. You know yourself in a way that is going to help people. You make others better because you truly accept them, no matter what. Even me. Even after I let you down.

Shelby's brother goes to your school, so I heard about what happened with the notes. If no one has told you this already, I want you to know I understand. It's hard to speak up when things are going wrong in your head. Sometimes you just want someone to notice that you're not okay. That feeling can make you do some pretty dark things.

Promise me you'll try really hard not to focus on the bad stuff. You have too much other, amazing stuff in your brain to get all blocked up with what hurts. I know it's hard to see all the good inside yourself. Maybe the hardest thing there is. But I know you can do it.

Just be you, Hannah. Spell your words and drop your pennies all over the place.

Look for me when you get to high school.

XOXOXO, Ashley


The first drops of snow fall from the sky above, and the air smells like new beginnings.

I gather a few flakes on my sleeve and let the crystals sparkle in the gray light.

"You are all special," I say.

"So are you," the flakes chime back to me like a choir, before melting away. But I know it wasn't really the snow telling me that.

If this were a story, then the main character would lie in the grass in her backyard and reread the letter from her pen pal, feeling full of her own kind of magic. It's not quite a happily ever after, but it's her ever after, and that's good enough.

# Acknowledgments

I want to thank my amazing agent, Zoe Sandler, at ICM for believing in this story; and my editor, Krista Vitola, whose guidance made this book a deeper version of itself. I'd like to frame all of your emails and hang them on my wall for inspiration. I'm so grateful for the chance to work with Simon & Schuster, and with both of you.

Thank you to my big family for their incredible support. Mom, Dad, and Crissy: This dream never felt impossible because I had you. Peace be the journey.

To my MFA colleagues, Writing Center family, and irreplaceable friends at Western Connecticut State University, there aren't words for how much you helped me grow as a writer and a person.

Zoe and Jess, thank you for being two of this book's first readers and for just about everything else. Ryan, everyone deserves a friend/personal hype-woman like you. Leo, thank you for coming to visit in that snowstorm and sitting there while this story spilled out.

And finally, but foremost, thank you to God for planting this passion in my heart and protecting me every step of the way.

Turn the page
for a sneak peek at
Beth Turley's next novel,

*The Last Tree Town*

Coming Summer 2020!

# Math in Real Life

On the first day of seventh grade, I calculate the distance between my sister and me. We're five miles (between schools) apart. If I missed her last year I would remember that she's somewhere in this building, speeding through a pop quiz or picking cheese off cafeteria pizza. But now a great wind has swept her twenty-six thousand four hundred feet away.

I dial the combination for my new locker. 13-27-51. It's been thirty-one days since I sat cross-legged and still on Daniella's comforter while she painted my nails sparkly blue. (Twenty-seven days of August, plus four days in July.) This can't be what teachers mean when they say we'll use math in real life. I stuff my binders in the locker and shut the door again.

Mr. Garrison, my sixth-grade algebra teacher, stands in front of me. His tie has division symbols on it.

"Congratulations, Cassi," he says in a voice like I've done something extraordinary. Much more extraordinary than making it to a new school year.

"For what?" I ask.

"Your grades from last year qualify you for Math Olympics." He hands me a fluorescent pink piece of paper. "What do you think?"

I think about sprinting up and down the hall and shouting *yes* as loud as I can.

"I'll be there," I say. I restrain myself from the sprinting and shouting, but can't stop the smile on my face. Even if it's been thirty-one days since I've seen Daniella's smile. Mom says we have the same one, sister smiles, but I think that's just because we both have crooked bottom teeth.

Mr. G high-fives me. Most of the blue paint on my nails has chipped off, but a heart-shaped speck still clings to my thumb. I use an old piece of tape to hang the fluorescent flier in my locker. Things look brighter now. For the rest of the day, I smile at it every time I take out a binder.

I find Mom in the kitchen after school.

"Mom, guess what?" I take the chair next to hers. Her fingers are wound up in her black hair. A newspaper sits on the table, opened up to the puzzle page.

*Red, puffy eyes + Unfinished Sudoku (difficulty level: 2 stars) = Nothing good.*

"Tell me, *mi amor*," she says. She writes *6* in a box.

"It can wait." I let my voice fade away. I fold over the edge of a placemat, a laminated parrot. We have a whole set of them. It's like our kitchen table is a bird sanctuary. "There's already a six in that row."

Mom sits in front of the blue jay. She studies the puzzle and then smiles at me in a watery way.

"Will you try to talk to your sister? I told your Dad to bring home her favorite pizza for dinner."

My breath catches.

"She won't listen to me."

"Please." Mom doesn't say it like a question. I

shove the chair back. The movement shifts the parrot, so it looks like it fell on its face.

Daniella's room is across from mine. Three feet apart. A sign on the door spells out her name in lavender seashells. We collected the shells in Mayaguez with Buelo and Buela, the town in Puerto Rico where they lived until Mom turned thirteen. I have a name-sign like Daniella's too. *Cassi* is spelled in pebbles.

I knock once, twice, three times. A shell is missing from one of the *l*s. I knock again. When she doesn't answer, I open the door. Daniella's door has a malfunction. The knob was installed the wrong way, so it only locks from the outside.

Her desk is straight ahead, overlooking the window. Daniella sits facing the sunset. She is bronze shoulders, yellow tank-top straps, dark curls hanging over the chair. A sister in pieces.

"Dinner soon," I tell her.

"Okay."

Her backpack spills out on the throw rug by her bed. I read the spine on one of the textbooks—*The Chemical Property of Life*. I want to ask her everything about her first day of high school, like if she got placed in American Studies and had the same lunch period as her friend Jenna. She told me she was worried about that.

"Dad's bringing Pepper's Pizza. Extra crispy, light cheese."

"*Okay.*"

The word cuts sharp, like stepping on a broken shell. I stop myself from thinking that Daniella is a broken shell. Because she's *not*. My hand hovers above the doorknob. I guess it doesn't matter whether something locks from the inside or outside. No one can get in either way.

# Pepper's Pizza

We sit at the table that night at our bird placemats. The pizza box is open between us. Pepper's Pizza puts a single red chili pepper in the center of all their pizzas. Daniella used to pick it off and wave it in front of my face.

*"Five dollars if you eat this," she said.*

*"Three days of math homework if you eat it," my sixth-grade self answered.*

*"No TV if you keep playing with your food," Mom chimed in. Dad nodded like he agreed but half-smiled while doing it.*

*Daniella and I paused for a second, giggles trapped in our throats, and then she popped the pepper*

*in her mouth, looking victoriously at me while she*
*chewed. Her dark brown began to water from the spice.*

*"Geometry for you," she said.*

Tonight the pepper sits on the pizza, curved like
a thin, red smile.

"Big day, *mi amor*," Mom says to Daniella. "High
school. Did you like your teachers?"

"Sure," Daniella answers. Her hand balls into a
fist on the toucan placemat. Her eyes are fixed on its
long, orange beak, like she wants it to say something.

"Did you find your way around okay?" Dad adds.

"Yes."

I stare so hard at the pepperoni slices on my pizza
that they turn to deep, dark holes. I want to disappear
inside one and end up in a world where Daniella still
dares me to eat spicy peppers.

"So a good day then?" Mom puts another piece
of pizza on Daniella's plate even though she hasn't
finished her first one. The red pepper flips over. It's
frowning now.

"It was *fine*."

Dad flinches. Mom opens her mouth and closes it
again. I think about the textbook on Daniella's floor.

Does *The Chemical Property of Life* explain how a sister can sit right next to you at a toucan placemat and still be disappearing?

I reach quickly for the pepper and scarf it down. It tastes like fire. Daniella looks at me for a second before turning back to the toucan. The kitchen is quiet with the sound of no one knowing what to say, like it has been for the last thirty-one days. I take a bite of my pizza and pretend the tears on my face are from the spice.

# Sunburn

My cousin Jac dyed her hair blue with Kool-Aid. She said a character in a book she read had done it, and that it was supposed to wash out in a week. It's been three. I sit outside the cafeteria at a picnic table with her and our friend Ben Chay. We get twenty minutes of free time after lunch. Free time, not recess. The late August heat presses down on me. I take off my cardigan.

"You even burn through sweaters," Jac says, and pokes my shoulder, where a red stain blooms across my ivory skin.

"So do you," I remind her.

"Yeah, but I don't have Puerto Rican genes." Jac

is Irish, like the other half of me. The half that presents itself through sunburns and sand-colored hair. Buela calls me *fantasma*, which means "ghost." *Take care of this skin, fantasma,* she reprimanded during our trip to Puerto Rico when I was nine, while she slathered my arms in SPF 70. Her accent wrapped around the word and made it sound pretty.

But I always noticed from my spot in the shade how Daniella's skin glowed when she laid on her striped towel, like she was made of gold and Mayaguez sunshine. I was made of white wispy things.

"Tell us about Math Olympics," Ben says. He shimmies to the song pouring out of his headphones, eyes bright brown and dark hair cut neat around his ears. Ben is going to live in a big city and be a star one day. For now, his talents are limited to local productions.

"It's boring," I lie.

"If it matters to you, it's not boring." Jac smiles. Her eyes flash and the corners of her mouth curve into her cheeks like carvings. She knows her smile is spooky and embraces it wholeheartedly. I think about Jac and Ben and Daniella and me sitting outside by the fire pit Dad built in our backyard. The last time we were out there, Jac had held a flashlight under her face and grinned.

*"You're supposed to say something, Jac. Tell us a story," Daniella said with a mouth full of s'more. The air smelled like smoke and summer.*

*"But are you not still scared?" she asked, letting her smile sink deeper.*

*"I am not."*

*Daniella laughed while Ben and I quietly compared our goosebumps.*

We called ourselves the Chordays, a combination of Ben's last name and ours, like we were our own family. Like a day of the week that no one knew about but us.

I shove away the thought.

"Okay, well, you can't join until seventh grade and we get together every week to practice different kinds of problems that might show up on the assessments and we take those and our correct answers get added together as a group and if we get enough correct answers then we can qualify for regionals and states and even nationals."

I run out of breath, like I've been underwater for a while. I have so many words built up because I didn't get to talk about Math Olympics at dinner last night.

"You're right. That is boring." Jac smiles again. The sun hides behind a cloud.

"Jac-lyn. Don't be mean to our genius," Ben says.

"Kidding! If I'm mean to the genius, who's going to do my algebra homework?"

"Maybe you?" he replies.

I laugh. Sometimes I wonder if Jac and Ben would be friends if they didn't grow up in the same apartment complex. Or if Jac and I would be friends if we didn't share an age and a last name. Or if Daniella only hung out with us because she felt like she had to. But maybe it doesn't matter how we all became friends or if we should've been. It only matters that we were. *Are.*

"Do you want to come over after school?" Jac asks. She pokes my sunburn again.

"I can't. We're visiting Buelo."

"Is Dani going?" Jac's eyes drop to the picnic table, like she might find Daniella there.

"She's supposed to."

Ben fidgets with his headphones. I do a quick calculation. It's been forty-seven days since that last night of s'mores and scary stories. The number forty-seven has too many sharp edges.

*"Are you going to forget us when you go to high school?"* Ben asked in his theater voice, a voice that can project all the way to the back row of an auditorium.

*"Hey."* Daniella held up her hand. *"You all can't get rid of me that easy."*

The bell rings to signal the end of free time. We shuffle like a herd back into Eliza T. Dakota Middle School. I want to stop thinking about the way Daniella looked at dinner, so different from that night around the fire. I focus on the back of Jac's head.

Her hair matches the sky.

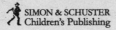

A magical wood,
a mystery, and an escape
from the make-believe . . .

SOME KIND
OF
HAPPINESS

Claire Legrand

Are the mysterious bottle messages Minna's
been finding under one of her town's three-hundred-
year-old bridges miraculously leading her toward the
long-lost answers she's been looking for?

Or are they drawing her into a disaster
of historic proportions?